Supernatural Community
Book Three

KRISTA STREET

Copyright © 2020 by Krista Street

Published in the United States.

All rights reserved. No part of this publication may be reproduced, scanned, transmitted or distributed in any printed or electronic form, or stored in a database or retrieval system for any commercial or non-commercial use, without the author's written permission.

ISBN-9798613533299

First Published: February 15, 2020

00 21 22 01 00

This book is a work of fiction. Names, characters, places and plot are either products of the author's imagination or used fictitiously. Any resemblance to any person, living or dead, or any places, business establishments, events or occurrences, are purely coincidental.

www.kristastreet.com

Cover art by: Covers by Combs

Also by Krista Street

Supernatural Community
Book 1 – Magic in Light
Book 2 – Power in Darkness
Book 3 – Dragons in Fire
Book 4 – Angel in Embers

Supernatural Standalone Novels
Beast of Shadows

The Makanza Series
Book 0 – The Second Wave
Book 1 – Compound 26
Book 2 – Reservation 1
Book 3 – Section 12
Book 4 – Division 5

The Lost Children Trilogy
Book 0 – Awakened
Book 1 – Forgotten
Book 2 – Remembered
Book 3 – Reborn

The Lost Children World
Book 1 – Retribution
Book 2 – Creation
Book 3 – Illumination

For the most up-to-date list of Krista's books, visit her website: www.kristastreet.com

Chapter 1

I screamed then screamed again.

Similar to my portal transfer to Emunda, the sound didn't carry, but I kept screaming.

I tried to curl into a ball but couldn't move. Jarring pain ripped through me as the portal threatened to shred my skin and crush my bones.

Somewhere in the swirling mess flew Daniel, the full-blooded angel accompanying me back to earth, but I couldn't see him. Nothing but blackness surrounded me.

I knew I was going to die. An image of my mother and my nan flashed through my mind.

I'll see you soon.

But just when I felt my ribs about to crack, the pressure stopped, and I landed. My legs buckled beneath me, and I fell on all fours.

My fingers sank into dry earth. Tall grass surrounded me. I panted loudly, my hands clinging to the dry, coarse stalks.

"Fucking hell," I muttered.

"Oh my. Did that not go well?"

I peeked up at the sound of Daniel's deep, musical voice. The angel towered above me. He stood at least six-three, his body sculpted and strong. His dark hair waved in the breeze as his turquoise eyes—the same color as mine—sparkled in the sun.

The *earth's* sun. Or at least, I thought it was the earth's sun. I relaxed my grip on the grass.

"Where are we?" Dirt crumbled beneath my knees when I shakily stood. A vast meadow surrounded us. Large towering oaks and aspens swayed in the breeze off in the distance. Bright sunlight filled the *blue* sky. I took that as a good sign. "We're on earth, right?"

"Of course." Daniel pointed at something far away. "The Supernatural Forces headquarters is just over there."

My heart leaped into my throat when I spotted the magical barrier, that glimmering red ribbon that only supernaturals could see. I tried to swallow my anxiety. The SF meant Logan—someone I did *not* want to see.

"Um, do we have to go there? I was kinda hoping to avoid that place."

"We need to inform your werewolf boyfriend—" He stopped when he caught my expression. "I mean *ex-boyfriend* that you are unharmed."

As I brushed the remaining specks of grass from my knees and clothes, my movements grew more agitated. "There are other ways to let him know. Like a phone call? You know, how Mother Nature intended we communicate?"

Merriment filled Daniel's eyes. "Ah, young angel, how amusing you're proving to be."

I forced a smile and waited to see if Daniel was going to push the matter because the last person I wanted to see was my werewolf ex-boyfriend and SF member, Logan Smith.

I shook my head. *I never thought I would be in this situation.*

Memories rose in my mind even though I tried to stop them. Only a few hours before, Logan and I had been enjoying a romantic afternoon in the supernatural marketplace, finally getting away from the headquarters. But all of that stopped when I'd spotted the psychic who had first alerted me to my dark angel power. And unbeknownst to me, when I went to search for her, Logan's fiancée had shown up and draped herself all over him like a tacky accessory.

The image of Crystal with Logan had seared itself into my mind like a brand. Of course, if I had known that Logan was engaged, I never would have considered him my boyfriend in the first place.

I snorted to myself. *What a liar.*

My heart rate increased as anger, pain, and the feeling of betrayal again fired in my gut. My dark angel power rolled in my belly, responding to my surge of emotion.

I concentrated on dusting my legs off and made a face at the mud stains on my thighs.

"Do you need to shower?" Daniel leaned over, his smooth forehead crinkling just enough to convey his concern. "That's the correct term, isn't it? To shower? How one cleanses oneself here on earth? Or do you still cleanse in rivers or perhaps a lake? Bathing varies from one culture to another, from what I recall."

"Yep, showering is one way Americans bathe." I eyed his pristine white pants. "But I see dirt doesn't affect you."

He just smiled serenely, the expression still making him look like a Calvin Klein underwear model. "I see that you're not only untrained in your powers but also in transferring between the realms. Shall we do it again? Would you like to practice portal transfer before we commence training on your powers? With enough practice, debris shall not bother you, either. Your clothing shall remain unaffected."

I backed up, waving my hands frantically. "Oh, no, definitely not. I'm very okay with *not* being well trained in traveling between the realms. In fact, I'd prefer to stay right here on earth, thank you very much, although the fae lands sound interesting. Maybe I'll go there someday, but not now. I think I'm all realm-traveled out for the time being."

Daniel's perfect white teeth flashed in a smile. "As you wish."

Scanning the meadow, I searched for the road. "Do you have any idea how to get back to Boise? I'm guessing we'll have to walk, but I really need to find Cecile and Mike so they know I'm okay."

Daniel pointed toward the trees. "These humans you refer to, Cecile and Mike, they're seated in a large box of some kind just over there. The box has wheels on the bottom and makes the most unpleasant sound when—" He tapped his chin. "What do humans call it? The *engine* starts?"

"Are you talking about the bus?"

"Ah, yes. The *bus*. That does sound correct."

I grinned. "Excellent! I can let them know I'm okay, then we can begin training." I set off through the meadow, the tall grass brushing against my thighs.

Off to the right, the magical barrier still glowed. I guessed Mike and Cecile had parked far enough away from the barrier that the sorcerer's mind-manipulation magic wouldn't affect them. Logan had said he would tell them where it was safe to park.

I stumbled as an image of Logan came unbidden to my mind—broad shoulders, dark hair, rich deep-brown eyes, and a chiseled body any woman would swoon over.

An aching gut-clenching sadness rose inside me. It was so sharp that for a moment, I couldn't breathe.

No! Don't think about him!

I shook my head firmly. Logan was with Crystal. Even if he was unhappy about that or didn't want to be with her, he didn't deny their engagement.

I forced myself to take a deep shuddering breath and welcomed the anger that burned away my sadness like fire.

Logan had tried to sugarcoat his engagement by saying Crystal wasn't his girlfriend, like using different terms to describe who she was somehow made his lying okay.

I scoffed. *Nice try.*

"Daria? A most unpleasant frown is upon your face again. Does the thought of seeing this Cecile and Mike distress you so?" Daniel strode at my side, his strong legs swishing through the grass.

I forced a smile and tried to bury any lingering memory of Logan, but my straining cheek muscles suggested that my smile most likely resembled a grimace. "Not at all. Cecile and Mike are like family to me. I was thinking about someone else."

"Ah-ha." Daniel continued gliding along as gracefully as a gazelle. "You were thinking of the ex-boyfriend werewolf who once held your heart dear."

I gave him a funny look. "Do all angels talk like you?"

He raised his perfect eyebrows. "Whatever do you mean?"

That time, my smile *was* genuine. "Never mind. But yes, if you want to know, I was thinking about Logan."

We reached the ditch and jogged down it. Since the road lay before us, I spotted the bus.

Cecile and Mike had parked a quarter mile away, in a sleepy-looking pullout. Nostalgia swelled inside me.

So much had happened in the previous weeks, and my life felt out of control. The thought of seeing Cecile and Mike and of sleeping in my own bed made my anxiety over what had happened with Logan lessen, if only a little.

Daniel effortlessly strode up the ditch to the narrow road. "Shall we meet with this Logan? If whatever occurred between the two of you distresses you so, perhaps a reconciliation is in line."

I snorted but swallowed the sound when I realized he was serious. "Um, no. If we can just concentrate on my training so I can control my angel powers, I'll be just fine never talking to Logan again."

He dipped his head. "As you wish."

I hurried down the road, brow furrowing, since Daniel kept saying, "As you wish."

Those were the exact words the vendor had spoken to me before I'd jumped into his shop's portal and landed in Emunda.

"Does that mean something among angels?" I asked. "To say 'As you wish'?"

He shrugged. "Not particularly, but it's a common phrase among our kind."

"Does that mean the vendor in the supernatural marketplace, the place I entered the portal to find you, knows about angels?"

"The vendor? Are you referring to Victor?"

"I don't know. Am I?"

"I believe Victor inhabits the place of which you speak. That portal is one of the few portals that accesses Emunda, and yes, Victor knows of angels."

"Does Victor have bushy eyebrows?"

Daniel's lips quirked up when we reached the bus. "His eyebrows do appear rather bushy."

"Then that's who showed me the portal." I sighed and reached for the release button on the bus's door. "In which case, the psychic who told me how to find Victor also knows about angels."

My frown didn't lessen as the door hissed open. It seemed that either the psychic I'd met during my teenage years was more than just a psychic, or she knew more than most supernaturals.

When I bounded up the bus's stairs to the living area, two sets of startled eyes met mine.

Cecile had been biting her nails on the couch but she jumped to her feet, while Mike tipped his Yankees cap off and stepped around the kitchen counter, his jaw dropping.

"Daria! You're safe!" Cecile covered the distance between us in one second flat and flung her arms around me, obviously not thinking.

My dark power rushed up, completely out of my control.

I lurched back, bumping into Daniel's hard form in my haste to get away from her. Already, the dark power was flowing down my arms toward my hands. Bad things happened when it reached that part of my body.

But the second I made contact with Daniel, something from him flowed into me. My dark power calmed. It retreated, as if yielding.

With a start, I realized the contact with Daniel had done it.

Daniel settled his massive hands on my shoulders. The further contact helped slow my pounding heart.

I closed my eyes.

Beneath his gentle touch, an indescribable feeling of tranquility and peace flowed along my nerves. *So this is what it feels like to be touched by an angel.*

"Dar? Are you okay?" Mike's worried tone had my eyes opening.

Cecile stood a yard away, a questioning expression fluttering across her face as she peered at Daniel.

The full-blooded angel gave me another brief squeeze before letting go and stepping back.

I missed his touch immediately, my dark power once again making itself known. That brief feeling of peace disappeared.

I cleared my throat. "I'm okay. Sorry if I worried you both. I didn't mean to."

Daniel continued wearing a neutral expression as his arms hung loosely at his sides.

"This is Daniel." I waved the introductions. "And this is Cecile and Mike."

Cecile nodded at him. "It's nice to meet you."

Daniel dipped his head. "The pleasure is mine."

Cecile's eyes widened at the sound of Daniel's voice. I smothered a smile. Considering that both Cecile and Mike were completely human, I wondered if they had any idea that they were speaking to a divine creature.

"Well," Mike said, scratching his head, "I have to say you're the first fella I've ever met who has the same eye color as Daria." He laughed. "And here we thought she was unique in that aspect." He stepped closer, peering into Daniel's irises. "Unless you're wearing contacts? Is your eye color real?"

Cecile swatted him on the shoulder. "Really, Mike. Where are your manners?"

Mike shoved his Yankees cap back on. "Sorry about that. Just took me by surprise. But you're the first person I've ever met who looks in any way like Daria. Of course, other than her mother." The second he spoke of my mom, a grief-stricken look entered his eyes.

I swallowed down the sadness that I always felt when I thought about her too. It was hard to believe an entire year had passed since she died.

"Anyway, as I was saying earlier . . ." I cleared my throat. "I'm sorry if I worried you. I'm guessing Logan told you he couldn't find me at the supernatural marketplace."

Cecile nodded. "Oh yes, he told us, and he's been frantically searching for you ever since."

"Speaking of Logan." My voice caught on his name. Just hearing it caused a tightening in my chest. "Will you send him a text and let him know that I'm fine?"

She frowned, her eyebrows drawing together. "You want me to text him? Don't you think we should go find him?"

"No." The word came out sharply.

Cecile frowned.

"Whatever had started between Logan and me is done. I don't want to talk to him. Will you please just text him and let him know I'm okay?"

Given the expression on her face, she obviously wanted to ask more questions, but she just nodded. "Sure, honey, but whatever happened between the two of you, you just let me know when you're ready to talk about it."

I was glad she didn't push me further for details. Already, my throat was closing, and the familiar longing returned.

Despite Logan's betrayal, I still missed him, and if I were being honest with myself—completely honest and not trying to bury how I felt—I missed him desperately.

Cecile sat back down on the couch and patted the cushion beside her. "Do you two want to sit? And are you ever going to tell us where you've been? We've been worried sick."

I sank down on the sofa next to Cecile, Daniel squeezing onto the cushion beside me. His thigh brushed mine, eliciting that calming feeling again as something from him flowed into me. My sadness lifted, serenity taking its place.

As odd as our meeting had been, I was coming to enjoy having Daniel around. He was like a personally tailored dose of Prozac and Ativan rolled into one.

I clasped my hands in my lap, trying to figure out how to explain my little journey from planet earth to Emunda.

"I was . . ." I tapped my chin. "I'm not really sure how to describe it, to be honest, but I'm okay now."

My phone vibrated in my pocket, and I pulled it out to see a call coming in. Logan's face flashed on the screen, and I sucked a breath in.

I hastily hit the ignore button, letting his call go to voicemail and was about to slip my phone back into my pocket when the date and time across the top of the screen caught my attention.

My jaw dropped. "I left over a *week* ago!"

But how can that be? Logan and I had ventured to the supernatural marketplace only that afternoon, following a Mexican lunch with Cecile and Mike.

I obviously hadn't received any calls or texts in Emunda, and as if just connecting to the mobile network, my phone dinged over and over.

Voicemails and texts rolled in. A quick scan through the incoming data revealed that most of them were from Logan. I shoved my phone back into my pocket. *I'll deal with that later.*

Cecile shook her head, her eyes widening. "How can you not know we've been searching for you for a week? We've all been so worried. The only reason Mike and I are here in the bus, and not out looking for you right now, is because Logan promised us he would track you down even if it was the last thing he did on this earth. We've been waiting close by ever since in case you returned, but until now, nobody knew where you were."

Mike stuffed his hands into his pockets. "You have no idea how relieved we are to see you, Dar. We were so worried that something bad happened to you."

"Well, nothing bad happened. I'm absolutely fine." My phone vibrated again, and my fingers itched to retrieve it.

Guilt filled me that Logan was so worried, but as soon as that feeling came, it went. I was no longer his concern. We'd broken up, and he'd lied to me.

But for some reason, despite telling myself that, I still

felt awful that he cared enough to keep trying to reach me.

"Just let him know I'm okay. Will you?"

Cecile pulled out her phone and texted Logan. Not even a second passed before her phone rang.

"Can you wait to talk to him until I'm gone?"

She frowned, reluctantly putting her phone away. "Regardless of whatever happened between you and Logan, you could've called to let us know that you were all right." Her scolding tone reminded me of my mother.

"I would have, but I couldn't, considering where I was."

Mike smoothed his bushy mustache. "Were you on Mars or something?" He laughed at his own joke.

"Close enough. I was with him." I hooked my thumb in Daniel's direction.

Returning her attention to the dark-haired angel, Cecile lifted a hand to her bun. "Of course. Daniel, was it? And you and Daria were doing . . ." Her eyebrows rose.

Daniel's sculpted lips lifted just enough to hint at a smile. "We were conversing, but now we have returned to this realm so that I may assist in her training."

Cecile and Mike just stared at him.

I leaned closer to him and said under my breath, "You really gotta stop talking like that if you don't want to draw attention to yourself."

Daniel arched an eyebrow. "Have I caused offense?"

"No, it's just that people don't really refer to earth as a realm. To do that is rather different."

He laughed, the musical sound filling the bus.

When I glanced back at Cecile and Mike, they were both staring at Daniel with slack jaws and glazed eyes.

I elbowed Daniel. "*And* you gotta be careful. I'm not sure if you appreciate the reaction you have on humans. Look what you've done to them."

Daniel cleared his throat, breaking the effects of his ethereal abilities.

Cecile and Mike shook their heads, as if coming out of a trance.

Mike's eyebrows rose. "What were you saying? Something about training?"

I gave Daniel a look. "We might as well tell them the full story. I mean, if that's okay."

The twinkle in Daniel's eyes grew. "As you wish."

Chapter 2

Similar to when Cecile and Mike had learned that Logan was a werewolf, they took the revelation of Daniel's angel status in stride.

Apparently, I wasn't the only one coming to terms with the increasing changes in our lives. Cecile and Mike had been forced to endure our new perception on reality as well.

"So what you're saying is that Faith and Alice, I mean Daria's mother and grandmother, were also angels." Cecile's gaze traveled between Daniel and me as we all sat on the couches.

"They were, weren't they?" I asked Daniel. "They both had turquoise eyes. Is that a sign of an angel?"

"It is. However, turquoise is not the only eye color of

angels. Lilac is another common shade among the divine."

Mike smoothed his mustache. "Well, I can honestly say that you're the first fella I've ever met with turquoise eyes, and I've never met anyone with purple eyes, so apparently, you're the first angel I've encountered. Apart from Daria, her mother, and her grandmother, that is."

Cecile jumped up from the couch. "I think I'm going to make a cup of tea. Would anybody like some?" She hurried off before anyone responded.

I watched as she strode away, her thin form stiff.

Guilt that I was responsible for this new stressor in her life, blowing her perception of reality once more, overwhelmed me. Cecile had been my mother's best friend, and she'd always believed my mother was human.

But there was no point hiding my lineage or that Daniel was an angel. His only purpose on earth was my training, and until I learned how to control my new dark power, we were all in limbo. Mike and Cecile depended on me to provide our living—Cecile as my manager, Mike as my bus driver.

Without Daniel's help, I would never be able to return to my livelihood as a supernatural healer. And since any future Logan and I had together ended when his engagement came to light, it seemed as if my old life was where I would eventually end up.

As much as knowing that hurt, healing was my destiny. My mom had said our lives weren't easy, that things would happen to make us question whether healing was a blessing or a curse. She said sacrifice was needed.

It was best that I remembered that and forgot all about Logan Smith.

"And there is that frown again, young angel," Daniel murmured, leaning closer. "What ails you now?"

I forced a smile. "Nothing." I jumped up from the couch. "Should we get to work on my training? Since I apparently lost a week in Emunda, we might as well get to it."

Daniel stood just as the teakettle whistled. "As you wish. Let the training commence."

∞ ∞ ∞

I landed on the ground—*hard.*

My uncontrolled dark power had once again knocked me off my feet.

Pain rocketed through my back as I lay like a starfish. For a moment, I couldn't breathe as I stared up at the blue sky in the meadow.

The sun had begun its descent, early evening arriving. After three hours of training, my control still hadn't improved, despite Daniel's coaching.

I stifled a groan of frustration.

If I step a bit more to the right next time, maybe I'll fall into the portal and travel to Emunda. Then I won't have to deal with this anymore. At least there my powers didn't bother me.

Never mind that I had no idea where the portal waited. Unlike the shimmery purple portal I'd seen in Victor's tent, I didn't see anything in the meadow.

I scowled. The fact that I was considering an "accidental" portal transfer to avoid learning how to control my dark power said something.

Finally able to suck in a deep breath, I groaned. "I don't know how much more I can take of this."

Daniel leaned over, hands on his knees, looking down at me sympathetically. The dying sun ringed the dark locks of his hair like a halo.

How fitting.

"You're trying too hard. Your powers and you are one. They are not separate. You must stop thinking of them as something in addition to your soul. Join with them. Become one. That is where you've been led astray."

He held out a hand, helping me to my feet.

Once standing, I dusted my shorts off. "Where's the portal, anyway?" I asked, looking around. "You know, in case I want to escape to Emunda to avoid any more bruised ribs."

"I'm afraid you are unable to realm transfer here."

"Say what? But this is where the portal returned us to earth."

"That is only because I commanded it so. There is no portal here. Emunda portals are rare, which is why Victor safeguards the one in the marketplace. I dare to say that most supernaturals are unaware of the land for lost angels, unlike the other realms."

I cocked my head. "I dare say you're right."

His lips quirked up. "Now, enough stalling. Let's return our attentions and energies to the matter at hand. You must halt your atrocious misgivings about storing your powers away."

"But my mom and my nan always said we had to call up our magic, and that when it's not being used for a healing session, that my inner healing light needed to stay locked inside me."

"While that is interesting, it is also grossly incorrect. I do not know of any angel that tries to contain their power."

I waved at the exposed skin on his forearm. "But you're containing your powers right now, right? Your skin isn't glowing, so aren't you controlling it?"

He glanced at his arm, his aquiline profile a perfect mixture of strong jaw and sculpted brow. The sight would have made any heterosexual female salivate, yet only an irritated grumble escaped me. He made controlling his angelic powers seem so easy.

"The only reason I'm not glowing at this moment is because I'm on earth. Glowing catches attention, does it not?"

I stretched my arms overhead, my muscles already stiffening. "Well, yeah. Humans don't glow, and neither do supernaturals—well, unless you're a fairy—but if you're not glowing, doesn't that mean you're controlling your powers, which kinda contradicts what you're telling me to do?"

I distinctly remembered the subtle glow of my skin in Emunda, when my powers had flowed freely just beneath the surface of my skin. There, Daniel's skin had glowed brightly too.

"No. I've simply tempered them so they're not as

close to the surface." Daniel spread his arms, and the glow suddenly appeared from his skin again. "Do you see my glow now? I am no longer tempering my powers."

Standing as he was, in the meadow filled with tall grass and distant trees, with his arms spread wide . . .

I sighed, my lips twitching up. "You look like the poster child for heaven."

He grinned just as his glow faded. I blinked, and his skin appeared like mine again, the glow gone. "See, young angel. I just tempered it. My powers still flow freely within me, yet slightly deeper so as not to cause alarm among your fellow humans."

I rolled my eyes. "Show-off."

"You shall learn too. With practice, your powers shall also flow freely. I fear the many years you've spent locking away your angelic light has taught you many bad habits. You must relearn to exist with your powers. Your angelic light and dark are meant to flow freely whilst you go about your daily existence."

"So you're saying my mom and my nan taught me wrong?"

He gave me a pacifying smile. "Perhaps not wrong. They simply led you astray."

I grumbled again. "Easy for you to say. You don't have to worry about blasting people to bits in Emunda."

"True, but I could 'blast people to bits,' as you say, here on earth, yet have I harmed your fellow humans in the *bus*? No. My powers are tempered, in sync with my soul. Now, shall we try again?"

"Can we give it a rest for a while? I don't think I can

take another landing like that last one."

"Perhaps you require sustenance? It has been a while since we have eaten."

My stomach growled, as if reminded of that fact. "Yeah, good idea. Dinner sounds like a much better plan."

"As you wish."

While Daniel and I headed back to the road, the barrier to headquarters still glowed in the distance.

I'd purposefully left my phone on the bus. Since learning of my return, Logan had already called three times, and that was before I shut my ringer off and threw my phone under my pillow.

So when we stepped out of the trees, the bus only a hundred yards away, I shouldn't have been surprised to see a tall, sexy-as-sin, and agitated male speaking with Mike and Cecile just outside of the bus's front door.

I ground to a halt, my stomach leaping into my throat. My hand shot out, stopping Daniel from progressing any farther. "On second thought, let's grab dinner somewhere else."

"Elsewhere?" Daniel eyed the bus, his turquoise eyes alighting in curiosity. "Ah, the werewolf ex-boyfriend has made an appearance. And from the looks of it, he seems intent on conversing with you at this very moment."

My heart thumped wildly. Logan had indeed spotted me.

Already, he was striding our way, a dark look on his face. His rich-brown hair, chocolate-colored eyes, strong broad shoulders, and tight square jaw made my heart pound.

Why did he have to be so good-looking, and *why* did my body have to betray me every time I saw him? Already, my core was clenching in desire, and he was still fifty yards away.

Logan's gaze swung to Daniel's, just long enough for his eyes to narrow.

"You know that idea about grabbing dinner elsewhere?" I asked, latching onto Daniel's arm. "How about we do that? Like right now? And can we take whatever portal you created? To somewhere? Anywhere?"

In an abrupt movement, Daniel swung me up in his arms, the propulsion taking me completely by surprise. "The young angel is requesting assistance. It is my pleasure to oblige."

Then the world turned into a blur. My breath caught in my throat just before earth once again disappeared.

Chapter 3

"What the hell just happened?" I asked when the world stopped spinning. I opened my eyes to see a small, plain, and dimly lit room.

Daniel cocked his head. "That was teleporting. That was what you requested, was it not?"

"Um, yeah." The only positive aspect about whatever portal transfer Daniel had just used was that in his arms, death didn't feel imminent. Held by him, I felt as if the journey had ended before it had begun. "Are we done?"

"Yes, young angel. The teleport is complete, and given your surprised expression, I am guessing this teleport went smoother than the portal transfers you previously suffered. Angelic teleportation and portal transfer aren't meant to be painful. We can add that training to the list of items you need improvement on. Should we not?"

"Yeah. Sure. Might as well."

He set me gently on my feet. I pushed my hair behind my ear, my head cocking as I took in the dim room, which looked vaguely familiar. "Where are we?"

"Victor's. The man with bushy eyebrows that you met before you commenced portal transfer to Emunda. And it is my understanding that the supernatural marketplace offers sustenance, does it not? Perhaps we could replenish our energy here. Besides, while my humanlike figure can blend in with the human masses, I have also been instructed by our maker not to draw attention to myself. The less I venture into populated human areas, the more likely I am to complete your training successfully whilst also pleasing our maker as I do His bidding."

I looked Daniel up and down. He was obviously delusional if he felt he blended in with *any* masses. "Right. Whatever you say."

It was all I could manage given the aftereffects of seeing Logan. I still reeled from how close he'd been.

Even though I'd been avoiding him in the few hours since my return, I hadn't expected him to show up like that. I swallowed down the butterflies that flapped in my stomach.

"Shall we journey into the marketplace?" Daniel pulled the curtain back, eliciting a startled shriek from the supernatural standing outside.

Victor rushed in, his bushy eyebrows shooting up to

his hairline. "My sir, my dear sir." He bowed deeply. "Forgive me for not knowing of your arrival. It is an honor to have you here. And please, forgive me, I did not know—"

Daniel held up his hand. "It is a pleasure to see you again as well, Victor, and forgive our intrusion. An unexpected visitor left my young angel friend in quite a state. We henceforth commenced an angelic transfer without properly alerting you to our plans. Forgive me."

"No, sir, no forgiveness needed." Victor rushed forward again, his blabbering words reminding me of teenagers throwing themselves at rock stars. "I'm happy to assist you in any way. Just tell me what you need." He bowed again then again, making me even more embarrassed at our unexpected arrival.

"We just came to grab something to eat." I stepped forward, peering out of the front of his shop at the busy marketplace. "Do you have any recommendations for a good restaurant? I mean, are there restaurants here?" I felt around in my pockets, shoulders slumping. "And do you maybe have a spare twenty bucks? I'll pay you back, promise. I just, ah, forgot my wallet."

"Bucks?" Daniel cocked his head.

"Dollars," I clarified.

"Of course." Victor bowed in my direction, making my cheeks flush again. "I'm happy to provide whatever you need." He reached into his pocket and extracted several bills before holding them out, bowing again.

I took them hesitantly. It all felt so wrong, like he thought we were royalty or something when I was simply a normal woman who happened to possess angelic lineage. Inside, I felt more like a woman than anything divine.

Pocketing the cash, I mentally reminded myself to pay him back. "Thank you. And I'll pay you back, even if you think it's not necessary."

After a very awkward goodbye, Daniel and I finally left Victor's shop to venture out to the marketplace. Of course, everywhere we went, supernaturals stared.

Even at the marketplace, Daniel stood out.

We finally found the café Victor recommended and grabbed a table. In no time, our order was in and our food served. I practically devoured the gyros that a band of gypsies with psychic blood had prepared for us. Licking my lips, I polished off the last bite.

"Has the sustenance replenished you, young angel?"

"Yes." I sighed in bliss.

Taking a sip of my drink, I leaned back in my chair, eyeing the serving counter again. Seeing the women behind the counter with their long dark hair reminded me of the psychic who'd told me how to find Daniel.

I set my drink down, clasping my hands on the table. "Do you think the psychic who told me about Victor also knows about my family's history?"

Daniel finished the last bite of his food, his square jaw chewing rhythmically. He held up a finger, letting me know he would finish chewing before he responded.

As I waited, a giggle drifted my way.

The group of teenage supernatural girls sitting near us once again made their presence known. I'd assumed they were witches, since they'd been practicing spells while eating their meals. But their spells seemed more like a way to draw attention, particularly one tall male's attention. However, the said male—the one with turquoise eyes, wavy dark hair, and perfectly symmetrical features—had barely paid them a passing glance.

The young witches batted their eyelashes at Daniel again before falling into a fit of giggles and whispered comments loud enough to make passersby on the street glance their way.

Daniel wiped his mouth, his long, elegant fingers making the very humanlike action seem as graceful as a dancer. "That is a fair assumption, dear Daria, considering this psychic knew of my acquaintance with Victor. Shall we search for her now that our energies have been restored?"

I nodded. "Yeah, I was thinking the same thing, since we're already in the marketplace and all." And that gave me an excuse not to train again until the next day. I rolled my sore shoulders. "I also can't help but think that knowing my family's history may help me understand why my dark power was locked away."

"As you wish."

We pushed away from the table, my chair squeaking against the floor while Daniel's seemed to glide in his grasp.

The young witches giggled again when we passed, one practically falling off her chair in her efforts to attract him.

On the street, I led Daniel back to the booth where

I'd first seen the psychic. Walking along the streets, smelling the scents of the marketplace, and passing shops I'd first visited with Logan made that damned aching sadness fill my chest again.

I fingered the necklace Logan had bought me. The cool onyx pendant sat beneath my shirt. I'd nearly forgotten I still wore it, given all that had happened.

Pushing thoughts of Logan away, I was about to round the corner to the adjacent street when a conversation drifted toward us.

"Red eyes on the vagrant. They said he . . ."

I stopped short, Daniel nearly colliding with me.

"Daria?" Daniel said.

But I was already retracing my steps, searching for the speaker who'd just spoken about red eyes.

I found him sitting at a bar, a crowd of supernaturals surrounding him.

"That's what me mate told me." His English accent grew thicker the closer I got. "Said a group of red-eyed fairies attacked the whole bloody group. Can you believe i'? I never 'eard of such a thing."

I pushed past the supernatural nearest the guy, my heart hammering harder. "Did you say red eyes?" I blurted.

The English fellow turned on his stool to face me. Five o'clock shadow graced his jaw, and considering his drink floated from the bar into his awaiting palm, I guessed he was a sorcerer. "That's righ'. The buggers had red eyes and attacked a group of me mates. What you know abou' i'?"

"Where did that happen?" I held onto the bar counter, the other supernaturals grumbling at my rude intrusion, but I couldn't help it. When Jayden and two other rogue werewolves had attacked me, they'd had red eyes too.

It couldn't be a coincidence.

The sorcerer summed up what he knew, but when he asked me why I was so curious, I was already racing back to Vendor 109's tent. Daniel glided behind me, his run more like a gazelle's than a human's.

"Young angel? Is it safe to assume we shall no longer be visiting the psychic you spoke of?"

"Not now!" I called over my shoulder just as Victor's tent came into view. My heart pounded from the run, but only one thought prevailed in my mind.

I had to return to the SF headquarters.

Wes needed to know that another attack had occurred and the red-eyed attack on me wasn't a singular incident.

Chapter 4

"How the hell do I get into this place?" If the headquarters' portal door actually had a door for me to kick instead of a glowing red barrier that was basically wavy light, I would have kicked it.

It didn't help that my irritation was running high. Daniel and I had teleported back to the bus then to the marketplace to repay Victor before venturing to headquarters. That diversion had added at least another fifteen minutes to our trip.

"Open already!" I yelled at the door.

The robotic voice repeated her rote statement for the third time. "Access denied. Should you need assistance from the Supernatural Forces, please contact your local agent."

I groaned. After trying repeatedly to enter headquarters at the portal door Logan had shown me, I'd once again failed, and I had no idea how to find my local SF agent.

Daniel arched an eyebrow. "Whilst I appreciate your enthusiasm for whatever it is you feel the need to convey to the SF, I must say, this is proving to be most ineffective. Perhaps a different approach?"

I stomped my foot, my fear over another attack that the SF might not know about making me desperate. "Can't you, like, use your angel powers or something and break into this place?"

Daniel held up his hands in surrender. "I'm afraid that would be most untoward and a gross misuse of my angelic abilities."

I was about to kick the wavy portal door again when the robotic voice abruptly exclaimed, "Daria Gresham and guest, welcome." The handprint screen glowed, making my eyes widen. "Please scan your palm before entering."

I slapped my hand on the screen and grabbed ahold of Daniel when the portal shimmered. "Follow me. We need to find Wes."

A moment later, we stepped out of the portal door, my hand still clasped in Daniel's. "On second thought, definitely add portal transfer to my training. It's much easier with your powers helping to—*oomph*."

I collided with a wall.

No, not a wall.

The sandalwood scent accompanying the wall made

me realize I'd walked straight into a chest—a very *male* chest that I'd grown achingly familiar with.

I sucked in a breath, my head tilting back to meet Logan's hard stare. His eyes glittered, his gaze traveling down my body, hesitating momentarily on my breasts, before trailing to my hand, which held Daniel's firmly.

His gaze stayed on Daniel's and my joined hands, a brooding scowl growing on his face. "So you're safe, and you're back from wherever you went in that portal." His nostrils flared. "And since you're here, I take it that you've finally decided to speak to me?" He finally looked up to make eye contact with me.

I held onto the angel with a death grip, Daniel's calming presence the only thing keeping me upright.

Why? Why? Why? Why did I have to run into him?

I couldn't handle seeing Logan at the moment. I was barely holding it together as it was.

It didn't help that up close, Logan looked exactly as I remembered him—a tall powerful frame, thick dark hair, smoldering eyes, shoulders so broad they brushed doorways, a square jaw, and a chiseled chest beneath his thin T-shirt.

Desire pooled in my core. He'd had that effect on me since day one, and betrayal or not, my body still recognized him as a potential mate. Not to mention that my nipples immediately hardened, as they always did around him.

I kicked myself mentally. Damned nipples. *Down, girls!*

"No. I, uh . . ." I cleared my throat. "I'm here to see Wes actually. Not you." I locked my jaw, my head lifting higher, but internally, I cursed my pounding heart.

A flash of pain washed across Logan's face. "Dar—"

"I just want to see Wes and then I'm leaving, Logan!"

His face hardened, and he stepped stiffly to the side. "I see. In that case, don't let me hold you up."

I paused, hating how much his brief pain-filled look affected me, but then I remembered that *I* was the one who had been hurt, not him.

"Welcome, Daria Gresham and guest. Please proceed to the identification processing room."

I sighed, thankful for the distraction. "Come on, Daniel. We need to check in." Turning swiftly, I pulled Daniel with me.

A curious glint tinted Daniel's turquoise eyes as he assessed the werewolf.

When Daniel and I passed, my hand loosened its death grip, as I'd expected Logan to return to wherever he'd been, but when his footsteps followed, I stopped and swung around. "We're fine, Logan. Daniel and I don't need an escort."

Logan put his hands on his hips. "How do you think you got in here? I cleared your admittance. Therefore, per protocol, I'm required to stay with you and your—" He swung his hard stare toward Daniel. "Speaking of which, who are you?"

"I am Daniel."

That was all he said. No handshake. No further greeting. Obviously, introductions in the divine realm were a bit lacking.

Logan's gaze narrowed. He stepped closer to my side,

his head dipping down. "Is this where you've been? Shacking up with this guy for the past week as you hid from everyone?" Bulging veins sprouted in his neck. His anger reminded me of how he'd been in the windowed image Daniel had shown me in Emunda.

"We haven't been shacking up, but yeah, I've been with Daniel for the past week."

Logan jerked upright, his breath coming faster. "It's good to know the past week has been so"—his gaze raked Daniel up and down—"easy on you."

I rolled my eyes, hand on my hip, and seethed. "I'm sure *Crystal* was glad to have me gone, or have you conveniently forgotten about your fiancée again?"

A regretful look entered his eyes. "Daria, I wanted to explain. If you would only listen—"

"To what? More lies? Or more half-truths? Or whatever the hell you call it when you tell me you don't have a girlfriend because you're actually *engaged?*"

He raked a hand through his hair. "It's not that simple."

"Really? Cause those kinds of things are usually *very* simple. You're either in a relationship or you're not, and being engaged is most definitely a relationship." My heart beat faster. I hated how much my pain was showing, but dammit, he'd broken my heart. I'd fallen in love with him, and he'd lied to me about everything.

Still, I hadn't meant to get into it with him, especially not in an SF hallway. I'd only wanted to find Wes, then leave.

That was it.

But I couldn't stop the volatile emotions swirling through my veins. At least Daniel was near and still holding my hand, otherwise, I felt fairly certain the dark power would have exploded.

Logan stepped closer to me but then cast an irritated glare toward Daniel.

However, the angel remained oblivious, making no move to back off or give us some privacy.

Nostrils flaring, Logan swung his glittery gaze back my way. "I know you're angry, and you have every right to be, but you shouldn't have run off like that. You've had everybody really worried. Do you even know how many times I've been back to the marketplace, visiting that vendor who's guarding that portal the SF knew nothing about? And did you know that vendor wouldn't tell me anything? Or that I've been going out of my fucking mind trying to find you?"

I scoffed. "Sorry. Next time I'll stick around to have tea and crumpets with you and your fiancée. Would that have been a more acceptable reaction for you?"

Logan raised his gaze skyward. "For fuck's sake, Dar." He lowered his head and pinched the bridge of his nose. "I was just saying that running off like that was really irresponsible. Do you have any idea how worried I was? Or how Cecile and Mike felt?"

I bristled. He actually thought I'd hid from everyone for a week *on purpose*. "I didn't know that I was going to be gone so long. I never would have done that to Cecile or Mike intentionally, and as for you . . ." Tears stung my eyes despite trying valiantly not to give a shit. I blinked them back as fast as I could, but I wasn't fast enough.

Logan took another step closer, his eyes remorseful, his face pained again. "Dar, please, give me a chance to explain what—"

"Welcome, Daria Gresham and guest. Please proceed to the identification processing room."

I jumped. *Saved by the bell.* "I think I saw enough of an explanation when Crystal showed up." I tugged Daniel again. "Come on, let's go. We need to find Wes, and I'm not interested in hearing any more lies." My hand tightened around my angel companion's, and I marched down the hall.

Daniel followed, his quiet, serene energy drifting into me.

Both his presence and his touch kept my erratic heart from leaping out of my chest. Just seeing Logan, talking to him, hearing his voice, and smelling his scent made my head swim and my heart ache. Even though he still seemed to care for me, I couldn't forget that he'd deceived me.

I *wouldn't* forget.

I took a deep breath, my feet tapping down the hallway in staccato beats. Similar to the entry bay where SF members entered through the portal door, gray walls and a concrete floor surrounded us. Everything about headquarters felt like a bunker or a military base.

A few steps later, we emerged in the identification processing room. Like my last visit, a handful of people appeared hard at work. A long workstation ran along the perimeter of the circular room. Several technicians sat in front of computers with holographic screens.

In the center of the room, a holographic display flashed brilliant colors and showed various areas of the world. The images continually changed, glimmering from one city to the next as beacons lit up, identifying individual SF members.

"Interesting." Daniel halted, taking in the scene.

"Daria! You're back!" Millie pulled off her headset and rushed over. An SF uniform covered her plump build, and her cherub cheeks lifted when she smiled. Her curious hazel eyes drifted to Daniel. "And you've brought a guest. Are you vouching for him, Logan?"

"Yes," Logan replied in a clipped tone from behind me. "I'll be escorting Daria and her *guest* today."

I ignored him and addressed Millie. "We just need to see Wes. I overheard something in the marketplace, and it's important that he hears about it."

"The marketplace? Is that where you went after you disappeared from the bus two hours ago?" Logan stepped closer to my side. "After your *guest* swung you up in his arms, I searched for you but couldn't find you anywhere." He squinted. "How did you get to the marketplace and back here so quickly? Did you use portal keys?"

Logan's scent drifted my way, flooding my nostrils and making my head spin. I gripped Daniel's hand harder. The angel didn't flinch, even though I was sure I was cutting off his circulation.

"No," I replied, "We used . . ."

I wasn't sure whether the way Daniel had teleported us from thin air was a secret or not, and I wasn't about to get on Daniel's bad side, even though the angel seemed as even-tempered as a basset hound—not like the overprotective and volatile werewolf in front of me.

Luckily, Millie saved me from having to explain further.

"Can you both hold out your wrists?" Millie lifted her scanning tablet, a pleasant smile on her face. Her sweet tone cut through the tension surrounding Logan and me like a knife.

I exposed my inner wrist, allowing Millie to point her tablet at my bare skin. An eruption of lasers emitted from the device. Following that, a warm tingling sensation shot up my arm before a symbol glowed on my wrist briefly before disappearing.

"Still a witch." Millie winked. "And you?" A rosy blush filled her round cheeks when she held the tablet up to Daniel.

Daniel cocked his head curiously and held his arm out like I had.

The lasers scanned his wrist. An alarm blared from the tablet, getting a jump from Millie.

"That's weird," she said. "It didn't identify you. No matter. We'll try it again." She positioned the tablet more carefully over Daniel's blemish-free skin and scanned his wrist again. The same alarm followed.

Millie shook the device. "Did this thing suddenly break?"

I wrung my hands. "Daniel's a . . . um . . . species that the Supernatural Forces may not be familiar with."

Logan's eyebrows drew together before he crossed his

arms. He leveled Daniel with a heavy stare. "What species are you?"

"Angelic."

Millie's eyes widened. "As in . . . an angel?"

Daniel smiled, his beautiful lips parting as pure radiance shone from his face. "That is correct."

A faraway look entered Millie's eyes as she soaked up the sheer power of Daniel's presence. The angel directed all of his divine charm entirely at the fairy. Millie swayed, a syrupy grin lighting her face, her tablet forgotten.

"Daniel!" I hissed under my breath. "Stop that. We need them functioning and of sound mind if they're going to help us."

Daniel straightened, his smile vanishing. "Have I caused offense again?"

"No, you're just . . ." I sighed, gripping his hand again as Millie shook herself, regaining her wits. I gentled my tone. "If you're going to train me, you need to comprehend the effect you have on people and supernaturals—"

"Train you?" Logan cut in. "What are you talking about?"

I opened my mouth to tell him, but just as quickly, I snapped it closed. "Nothing. Never mind."

But one thing had become apparent from my identification processing. I was definitely part witch according to the SF, which explained my ability to cast spells with telekinetic witch magic. But like Daniel, the SF had never identified my angel lineage.

I shook myself, knowing at the moment, that wasn't

important. "Can we see Wes now?"

Logan's brow furrowed, his gaze swinging between Daniel and me again. I could tell he wanted to ask more questions, but Millie interrupted. "Are you going to take them, Logan?"

Turning stiffly, Logan walked toward one of the halls. "Yes, I'll take them. Follow me."

∞ ∞ ∞

"So you're telling me that a sorcerer in the Lupine for Life bar said one of his friends was attacked by red-eyed fairies?" Wes stood in one of the SF conference rooms, arms crossed, a heavy scowl on his face.

Similar to Logan, thick muscles covered his body, but unlike Logan, gray hair covered his head. He began to pace, his brow furrowing.

A loud hum emitted from the air conditioning, cool air swirling in through the vents, but it wasn't loud enough to hide Wes's sharp growl. He snapped his tablet off his belt and hit a few buttons.

"Millie. Get a team to the Lupine for Life bar now." He rattled off the description of those I'd spoken to. "Bring them in for questioning."

After he finished dispatching, he paced the length of the conference room. "That's the second attack this week, only we never heard about that one. Whoever was attacked must not have reported it."

I leaned forward in my chair. "There was another one?"

Wes eyed Logan, his expression clouded.

Logan straightened, tense energy pooling around my ex-boyfriend. Though I'd tried to put distance between Logan and myself, he had insisted on sitting at my side. Daniel occupied the chair on my other side, while the remaining twenty seats around the large boardroom table stayed empty. Wes had stood the entire time.

"What second attack, Logan?" I asked when Wes didn't seem intent on answering me.

Logan cleared his throat, his attention on his superior. When Wes gave him a curt nod, Logan replied, "Another attack happened four days ago in Virginia. Three supes—a psychic, a witch, and another rogue—attacked a family camping in the Great Smoky Mountains. The father was an elite SF member, one of our best. He was on leave for a family vacation. His wife and children were killed. He barely made it out alive. If he hadn't, we'd have never known about the red eyes."

I sucked a breath in. "His family was killed?" My hand flew to my mouth, tears springing in my eyes. Only last year, my entire family had also died. The pain was still fresh despite an entire year passing. "That poor man. He must be devastated."

Logan's head dipped. "He is. After he relayed what happened and helped at the crime scene, he went home. He hasn't left his house since and won't speak to anyone."

I held back the tears that wanted to drop onto my cheeks. I understood his devastation all too well.

Daniel placed a hand over mine. I closed my eyes,

letting his angelic touch heal the hurt and pain. I squeezed him back. When I opened my eyes, I blinked, the tears gone, but when I turned to ask Logan more about the incident, I stopped short.

Logan sat completely immobile, his gaze glued to my and Daniel's hands. An aggrieved expression filled his face.

He lifted his eyes to mine, warring emotions swimming in his irises. "So you really can touch him despite the dark power? You've been touching him all evening." The pain in his eyes increased. "So his touch doesn't bother you even though mine did?"

A memory brushed my mind—Logan and me in bed, a feather, a blindfold over my eyes, and delicious sensations coursing through my body.

My lips parted, and I cleared my throat. "No, his touch doesn't bother me."

A fierce growl tore from Logan, and he snapped his gaze away. With a start, I realized that Logan had interpreted that as Daniel being another potential mate, one who *could* touch me despite my dark power.

My heart beat harder, but I didn't correct Logan. Instead, I reminded myself of Crystal and lifted my chin.

Logan's breath sucked in, and he abruptly pushed back from the table, the wheels under his chair swiveling erratically. "Excuse me, Wes. I need to step out for a minute." With stiff movements, he strode from the room.

I swallowed around the lump in my throat. The agony that had etched so deeply in Logan's face had rivaled an ocean trench. My heart thumped wildly, unsteady breaths lifting my chest.

"Daria?" Wes asked quietly. "Are you all right?"

I cleared my throat. As much as I didn't want to care, I wasn't fooling anyone. I still cared, *so much*, more than I wanted to. "Is Logan okay?"

Wes sighed heavily. "It's been a tough week for him, and you going missing didn't help matters. He has . . ." Wes cocked his head. "How do I put this? He has some stuff going on with his pack that's taking a toll on him."

Stuff with Crystal?

But I didn't ask, and even though Logan had betrayed me, that glimpse into his inner turmoil still shook me. Despite trying *not* to feel it, guilt filled me. I'd just added to Logan's pain.

My mouth suddenly felt dry. "Is there anything I can do to help with your investigation into the red-eyed supes?"

"I would still like to understand how you killed those rogues. If you're up for it, I would appreciate your input. Master Gregor has been searching through scrolls, and I believe he's found a few things."

"But I already know how I killed those rogues." I glanced at Daniel. "It was from my angel powers, my dormant angel power."

"Angel power?"

Rubbing my hand on my shorts, I said, "I'm apparently half angel. That's how I killed those rogues. It wasn't witch magic."

Wes cocked his head then looked at Daniel then me, for the first time *really* looking at us. "You have the same eye color."

I nodded. "Apparently, it's an angel trait."

Wes shook his head. "So we can't replicate what you did for other witches to use?"

"I don't think so. At least, I'm pretty sure we can't, unless they're also part angel."

Wes raked a hand through his gray hair. "So much for that idea."

My feet jittered under the table, and I cleared my throat. "So . . . what did Master Gregor find?"

"I don't know the exact details yet, but you can stop by to see him before you leave." Wes reached into his pocket and withdrew his phone. "I'll call Logan back to escort you to the library before you leave for the night."

I took a deep breath, picturing Logan striding back into the room, and gave a shaky nod. "Okay."

Chapter 5

After Wes exchanged a few texts with Logan, Daniel and I waited in the conference room for my ex-boyfriend to return, while Wes busied himself on his tablet.

I bounced my knee under the table. The memory of the turmoil and pain on Logan's face before he'd walked out continually assaulted me. What the heck was going on with his pack? I knew he'd joined the SF to escape his duties at home, but why would he be engaged to Crystal if he actually wanted *me?* He certainly wasn't acting like someone over me, and if that were the case, why not just break up with Crystal? It didn't make any sense.

I bit my lip, for the first time wondering if I should have heard him out.

Behind me, the door opened, *whooshing* against the

carpet.

I swung around, my stomach flipping as I thought about all the things I wanted to say to my ex-boyfriend but wasn't sure if I could.

But my stomach plummeted when Brodie, Alexander, and a woman I didn't recognize sauntered into the room.

Brodie and Alexander, two of the werewolves in Logan's SF squad, were also his pack brothers from Wyoming. As for the woman, I had no idea who she was.

Brodie put his hands on his hips before saying to Wes, "Logan just called us about Daria and her friend needing an escort. Logan's busy at the moment, but we can take them to wherever they need to go."

"Very well." Wes holstered his tablet. "Will you take her and Daniel to the library to see Master Gregor?"

"You got it, boss." Brodie pretended to tip a hat he wasn't wearing.

Alexander nodded in my direction, respectfully acknowledging me. He then assessed Daniel, his mouth thinning. "Do you want to follow us, Dar?"

The woman who stood beside them watched all of us with piercing blue eyes. Long jet-black hair draped down her back, and a stud pierced her nose. Despite her porcelain skin and delicate-looking hands, toughness exuded from her, the image helped by her shit-kicker boots and tall stature. She had to be at least five-ten.

"You're the healing witch?" the woman asked, crossing her arms.

"That's me." I stepped closer to her. "Have we met?"

"Nope. I'm Xanthia Cummings. Nice to meet you."

She held her hand out, and her full lips stretched, revealing straight white teeth. The grin transformed her, removing the hard edge to hint at soft beauty that she seemed intent on masking.

I eyed her hand apologetically. "Sorry, but I don't shake hands."

Xanthia let her hand fall. "Oh, right. Logan mentioned that."

Hearing Logan's name made my heart skip, but I pushed it down. "Logan mentioned you to me too. You're the dragon trainer from California, right?"

"That'd be me."

"Say, Dar? You gonna introduce us?" Brodie asked, placing his hands on his hips, which made his balled shoulders press against his shirt. His icy-blue eyes slid over Daniel.

"Oh, right." But before I could get to it, Daniel stepped forward.

"I am Daniel."

"You are Daniel?" Brodie's eyebrows rose as he eyed the tall angel.

"Yep, he's Daniel." I figured there was no point trying to explain Daniel's lack of human niceties.

"Okay then." Brodie shook his head. "Should we head to the library?"

Xanthia's long arms brushed against her sides when the five of us stepped back into the hall. Daniel glided beside me, but his gaze kept straying to Xanthia.

"Something you'd like to ask?" She glanced his way, an edge to her tone.

Daniel dropped his turquoise gaze. "Forgive my curiosity. I've simply never encountered a dragon trainer before. I've only heard of your kind."

"Her kind?" I had to look up at both of them since everyone in the group was at least six inches taller than I was.

"Xanthia's half demon." Alexander shoved his glasses up his nose and brushed his shaggy brown hair out of his eyes. "You have to be a demon or half demon to train dragons."

I nodded. "Right, I think I remember that, but why is that?"

We rounded a corner in the long concrete hall, the humongous double doors to the library just up ahead.

Xanthia stuck her tongue out, rolling a tongue piercing between her teeth before she replied, "Because dragons guard the gates to hell, and to train them, you have to be able to live there." She grinned at my horrified expression. "Only those with demon blood can tolerate the heat."

∞ ∞ ∞

Concentrating on my upcoming meeting with Master Gregor proved challenging after learning details of Xanthia's occupation. I kept picturing huge, scary, fire-breathing dragons in front of thick black gates in a fiery inferno.

Of course, I had no idea if that was what the gates of hell looked like, but my imagination gave me plenty of material to work with.

When we stepped into the massive library, Master Gregor hobbled toward us, his grotesque gargoyle face the thing of children's nightmares. His wide mouth, gaping teeth, and stone-like skin were akin to something from another world. "Daria, what a pleasure to see you again!"

"Nice to see you too." I smiled down at the four-foot scholar. "Wes said I could see you again before I left for the night."

"Of course. Follow me."

The library rivaled the size of a football stadium and had a ceiling that was at least a hundred feet tall. Rows and rows of shelves, stacked higher than seemed humanly possible, towered all around the room. The sheer size of the cavernous room was shocking enough, but the fact that the middle shelves floated would make any newcomer pause. Each large floating shelf was thirty feet tall and swayed and moved in the air, as though they had life forces of their own.

I returned my attention to the scholar. "Wes said you found something about my family's history."

Master Gregor stopped and bobbed his head. "Yes, indeed, I have—" The gargoyle jumped, a delighted grin filling his face. "Oh my! Is that an angel you brought with you?"

"Angel?" Brodie's eyebrows rose.

"Oh, yeah." I stepped aside so he could see Daniel better. "Master Gregor, this is Daniel."

Master Gregor hurried over to Daniel, his grin

stretching even further. "Well, it's certainly a pleasure. I haven't seen one of you on earth in over a thousand years."

Daniel dipped his head. "The pleasure is mine."

"Wait." I frowned. "How did you know he was an angel?"

"Why, his power. Can't you feel it radiating from him?" Master Gregor replied. "I haven't felt power like that in over a millennia."

He can feel Daniel's power? Huh. The gargoyle had never detected my angel powers, though, but then again, I wasn't full-blooded.

Brodie put his hands on his hips, his eyes widening. He glanced at Alexander and Xanthia. "Did you know this dude was an angel?"

Xanthia fingered an ear piercing. Six studs wound up her earlobe. "No. I didn't know angels were allowed on earth."

Alexander peered at Daniel through his dark-rimmed glasses. "You and Daria have the same eye color."

"That is correct. Turquoise eyes are common among the divine," Daniel replied.

"Turquoise eyes are a sign of angelic lineage?" An excited expression grew on Master Gregor's face. "I wonder if that's recorded in the history books. If not, I'll record it today."

"Or lilac eyes," I chipped in, getting a smile from Xanthia. "That's an angelic eye color as well. I just learned that the other day."

"Huh." Brodie's gaze swung between Daniel and me.

"So that means . . . *you're* an angel too?"

"Well, part angel, as I came to find out this week, but it's a long story."

Brodie scratched his head. "But I thought you were a witch."

I thought about the simple spells and incantations I knew. "I am part witch too. I guess I'm a hybrid."

"Fascinating!" Master Gregor clapped his hands. "And a very interesting aspect of my studies! The fact that you've identified your lineage only further confirms what I found in my searches."

I took a step closer to him. "You found something about angels in your searches?"

Master Gregor nodded enthusiastically. "Come with me. I'll show you." He hobbled back to a floating shelf.

Even though I'd been in the library before, the towering shelf still made me gape when I stood right beside it.

Master Gregor waved his hand, and a floating ladder glided to him. He hopped onto it then quickly ascended the rungs before leaning precariously to one side to snatch several scrolls from the top shelf. Holding them tightly, he descended the ladder, his long claws grasping each rung carefully, before hopping back to the floor.

He held out the scrolls, and I sneezed. A plume of dust along with a musty smell wafted up from the parchment.

"Let me show you." Master Gregor beckoned us to a large wooden table that was about two feet tall, the perfect height for a gargoyle scholar hard at work.

Working the parchment carefully, he unrolled it, mindful of his large claws. "I found this last night." He beamed up at me.

I licked my lips, my breaths growing shallower as I bent down, scanning the scroll eagerly. But as before, the text flowing across it depicted a language I didn't know. "What does it say?"

"It says exactly as I suspected," Daniel replied, leaning over my shoulder.

"You can read this?" I glanced up at him.

"Of course. Can you not?"

"Angels are versed in many languages," Master Gregor cut in. "I'm not surprised your friend can read this text and has already spotted what I did. What it says here"—he tapped on the scroll, careful not to puncture the parchment with his claw—"is that you are a direct descendent of a full-blooded angel."

"I am?" Even though that information didn't shock me, my heart still thumped erratically. Finally, I was getting some *real*, documented answers. "What else does it say?"

Master Gregor leaned down, scanning the text. "It says that over fifteen hundred years ago, your maternal ancestor, a witch hailing from the Mediterranean region, fell in love with an angel. They had an offspring, a daughter, who inherited her father's powers, which solidifies that you are indeed part angel."

Mediterranean. In that part of the world, most people didn't look like me. I fingered my long blond hair. "What did he look like?"

Master Gregor peered down, his large black eyes scanning the scroll. "Ah yes, here it is. According to this, he looked just like you—blond hair, *turquoise* eyes, and pale skin. And considering that description is a near replica of you, I'd say his lineage still runs through your veins."

"And my distant grandmother, the one from the Mediterranean area? What did she look like?"

Master Gregor returned his attention to the scroll, Daniel and the others still hovering over us. "It says she had dark-brown hair, olive skin, and brown eyes." Master Gregor turned back to me. "But the coloring of your distant grandmother is of no consequence when dealing with angel blood."

Daniel stepped closer to the paper, his long, elegant finger pointing at a particular line. "He's right. This history solidifies that you are indeed of angel descent, and the fact that your distant maternal grandmother bred with an angel over a thousand years ago, yet you still carry his mark, proves that he was a very powerful angel."

I frowned. "His mark?"

Daniel nodded. "Dozens of generations remove you from your angelic grandfather, yet you bear his coloring and carry his potent powers, which means half of the blood swimming through your veins comes from him. Time hasn't diluted it. One could say that he's not really your grandfather at all but your actual father. You're most definitely half angel—and half witch, as inherited from the women in your family." He smiled, his breathtaking features softening.

"Does that mean that . . ." My throat constricted, and my mouth suddenly felt dry as I remembered a horrible encounter with a man who I'd thought was my father only weeks ago. "That Dillon Parker isn't really my dad?"

Master Gregor's eyes grew wide. "Yes! How very true!" He clapped his clawed hands, excitement shining in his dark eyes. "If she still carries angelic traits and is able to wield angelic power, half of her blood most definitely comes from her angelic grandfather, and like you suggest, he's almost like a father to her."

Daniel nodded. "It's fair to say that no human has ever been your father. They bear the seed to help the women in your family create a child, but their human genes are diffused out sometime in utero. The blood you carry is identical to the blood of your angelic grandfather."

I backed up, nearly tripping. Dillon wasn't my father? Dillon *wasn't* my father!

My shoulders shook, a sob of relief coming from out of nowhere. It hit me so hard that I fell to the floor.

"Whoa, Dar, hey . . ." Brodie kneeled at my side, looking entirely uncomfortable with my sudden emotional outburst.

I tried to wipe my tears away, but they still poured out despite Daniel leaning down to touch me.

"Here." Xanthia pulled a tissue from one of the many compartments of her cargo pants and handed it to me.

"Thanks," I mumbled. I blew my nose and hiccupped a few times. "I'm sorry, it's just that . . . Dillon Parker was such a—"

"Monster?" Alexander cut in.

I nodded vigorously. "So to know I'm not actually related to him, that I don't come from him, it's like such a relief. You know?"

"Oh, I get it," Xanthia replied. "My demon dad's not exactly an upstanding model citizen, if you know what I mean."

Her snicker made me smile before I returned my attention to Master Gregor and Daniel. "So that's why all Gresham women look identical? It's almost like we're *twins?*" I looked for a stool, feeling ready to pass out. "What the heck does that mean? That my mother was really my sister, and my grandmother was my sister too?" It was too foreign and bizarre for me to understand.

Daniel swung me up into his arms and carried me to a large wooden chair, dodging underneath a floating shelf as it zipped to the other side of the room. He set me down, the hard wood of the rather uncomfortable, if ornate, large chair poking into my back.

He crouched in front of me again, taking my hand. When he entwined his fingers with mine, Alexander and Brodie shared confused looks.

"In a way, yes, I suppose they were more like sisters to you," Daniel replied, "but your personalities were different, were they not? Despite sharing identical blood and genetic lineage, you are still your own person."

My breaths came faster even though Daniel did his best to calm me.

Brodie raised a hand, skepticism glittering in his eyes. "Wait, wait, wait. So you're not only telling us that Daria is an *angel*, but you're also saying that her angelic blood is so potent that it doesn't dilute with matings?"

"That's exactly what we're saying," Daniel replied. "Daria, her mother, her grandmother, and all of the Gresham women that came before her were half angel. And given the potency of her distant grandfather's blood, I would further guess that he was one of the original angels. While angelic blood can show this kind of strength over time, the fact that it has not diluted in the slightest in over fifteen hundred years leads me to presume that he was an archangel."

My mouth went dry. "An archangel? Why didn't you tell me that before?"

Daniel shrugged. "I didn't realize that he was so distant in your family's lineage. If I had, I would have informed you."

"That's rad." Xanthia crossed her arms. "I'm half demon, but that's only because dear old Dad is full-blooded. I don't know if I've ever heard of demon blood carrying that kind of strength after so many generations."

"No," Master Gregor agreed. "Only angel blood carries that kind of power. Demon blood, even full-blooded demon blood, is unable to be passed down following the first generation. If you ever have a child, Xanthia, with a species other than a demon, your child will not carry any demon blood, only your mother's psychic blood. In other words, your children will never be able to train dragons."

Xanthia rolled her eyes. "Yeah, I know, my mom told me the same thing, but aren't I a bit young to be contemplating whether or not I'll bear demon spawn?"

Alexander snort laughed, his eyes twinkling when he looked at Xanthia.

"So do angels and demons get along?" I asked Daniel.

Daniel's eyes widened as an offended expression flitted across his features. "Most certainly not. Demons are our archenemies."

I shifted my weight in the chair, glancing nervously at Xanthia. "You don't seem to mind Xanthia, though."

"She is of demon descent—that is correct—but as a half demon or youngling of a full-blooded demon, she does not carry all of the attributes of her father. It's quite possible that there is goodness in her soul, even kindness. Only full-blooded demons are pure evil. They are our only true enemy."

"Thanks for that, Angel Boy," Xanthia replied sarcastically. "It's good to know I don't carry the sins of my father."

Alexander and Brodie laughed.

"So is there anything else in there about my family's history?" I peered at the scroll again. "Does it talk about my powers or how my ancestors had both dark and light? I still don't know how my family suppressed the dark power or why it disappeared."

Master Gregor clapped his hands. "Oh my goodness. Of course! I almost forgot the most interesting part!" He trailed his claw-like finger down the parchment again, nearing the bottom. "It says here that your ancestors once possessed both the dark and light powers, as I told you the other week, but this particular text goes into even more detail. It speaks of how your ancestors sought to rid themselves of their dark power after several generations of employment in a position they did not wish to continue."

I scrunched my eyebrows together. "What does that mean?"

Master Gregor's eyes dimmed. "It seems that a ruler long ago in Europe took advantage of your family. Once word spread of the Gresham women's healing powers and their ability to banish evil and kill with one touch, they became targets. This particular ruler forced them to use their dark power to do his bidding. He made them kill."

I gasped. "To kill? Are you kidding me?"

"Sadly, no. For many generations, the Gresham women weren't just healers. They were also executioners."

Chapter 6

"I think I'm going to pass out."

I swayed back on the chair, but Daniel grasped my hand tighter. His soothing touch blanketed my soul, stopping the sick churning in my stomach and helping to clear my head.

"Shh, my young angel."

I leaned forward, taking deep breaths. "My family was executioners? Seriously? Freakin' *executioners?*"

The dark power swirled, intrinsically responding to my fear and anxiety.

I gripped Daniel's hand more. He slid his warm, smooth fingers through mine. Something from him flowed into me, and his light touch halted the progression of my uncontrolled power.

Brodie frowned, his gaze once again straying to our entwined fingers.

He and Alexander shared more troubled looks. Brodie crossed his arms over his massive, muscled chest, his aggrieved expression growing.

"So what happened to all of my ancestors that were forced to kill?" I asked Master Gregor.

Master Gregor kneeled at my side. His large black eyes, while scary to look directly at, took on a twinge of sympathy and regret.

"Unfortunately, this particular scroll doesn't go into great detail about that time in your family's history. All it says is that for several generations, your family was forced to use their powers to kill men and women who were sentenced to die. But then it abruptly stops with one generation, saying they no longer had their dark power. After that, it simply says the Gresham women disappeared from Europe. I'll keep searching for further information about your family, but my guess is they went into hiding. Where they went following those troubled centuries, I don't know."

I took in another shuddering breath, trying to picture my dark power being unleashed upon an unsuspecting human.

I held onto Daniel like a lifeline as my stomach rolled and was thankful when his touch provided soothing relief from the dark power and helped keep the nausea at bay.

"Do you know anything about what happened to them?" I asked him.

Daniel shook his head. "If I knew, young angel, I

would tell you."

"Is there a way for you to find out?" I asked Master Gregor. "I feel like this may be the key to understanding my powers. If something happened that banished the dark power from my ancestors around that time, that could explain everything."

"I will keep searching." Master Gregor hobbled back to the table to roll up the ancient parchment. The tall floating shelves continued to glide around the room, as if shifting in a breeze no one else could feel.

"Will you tell me what you find?" I asked anxiously.

"I will report all findings to Wes, as the courts have instructed me." Master Gregor smiled, his gaping mouth revealing rows of sharp teeth. "Although I'm sure the SF general would be more than happy to share that information with you."

My shoulders slumped with relief, yet I still nibbled on my lower lip. I tried to imagine what it would be like to harness the dark power for malicious intent, to use my gifts for a power-hungry ruler's sick ambitions.

Daniel gripped my hand more firmly, as if sensing my emotions, before he transferred both of his hands to my shoulders. A strong soothing power ebbed from him into me.

I closed my eyes, and the nausea completely disappeared. With relief, I opened my eyes, giving Daniel a grateful smile.

Brodie grunted. "You ready to get out of here, Daria?" he asked gruffly.

I snapped my attention to him, startled by his sharp

tone. "Yeah, of course. I'm sorry to hold you guys up. I know it's getting late."

After thanking Master Gregor for his time, I followed Logan's pack brothers, Xanthia, and Daniel from the room, my heart heavy as thoughts of my ancestors' pain rolled through my mind.

But when we reached the elevators that would take us to the portal exiting the headquarters, my steps slowed. Realizing I was about to leave without knowing what had happened to Logan, I ground to a halt.

"Can you tell me how Logan's doing?"

Brodie and Alexander shared those looks again, a look veiled with concern and something else . . . *Anger?*

"He's fine, Daria. Don't worry about him." Alexander pushed the button on the elevator.

I stepped closer to his side, my powers safely locked within, thanks to Daniel's soothing touch. "He didn't look fine when he left the conference room earlier. He looked upset."

Brodie scoffed. "Why do you care?"

I snapped my head back. "What does *that* mean?"

Brodie rolled his eyes. Gone was the joking, laughing Brodie that I had known from our previous encounters. A hard edge filled his words. "You broke his heart, Daria."

My jaw dropped as the elevator door dinged open. Alexander tried to shuffle me into it, but I held my ground. "*I* broke *his* heart? He was engaged to somebody else and lied to me about it, and you have the audacity to say that *I* broke *his* heart?"

"Look, Daria," Alexander cut in, "I get it that you're angry. I really do, but you don't know what's going on with our pack, and you definitely don't know Crystal's history with Logan."

"Well, of course I don't," I retorted. "Because nobody's ever bothered to tell me!" My chest rose and fell quickly as the elevator door dinged closed, though nobody stepped aboard. "How am I supposed to understand something that nobody will explain? And now, you're all blaming me for Logan being hurt, when he's the one who deceived me!"

"Well, you certainly moved on fast enough," Brodie said under his breath. "I don't know why you give a shit anymore."

"Did you just say that I've moved on?" I planted my hands on my hips, my eyes narrowing. The dark power rolled violently, but I stepped closer to Daniel, brushing my arm against his so it wouldn't grow out of control.

Brodie's gaze dipped. He waved toward my and Daniel's arms. "Yeah, moved on. You disappear for a week, scaring the shit out of everybody, only to turn up with this dude, your new boyfriend. And then you go and rub it in Logan's face when it's obvious to anybody that the dude's been scared out of his fucking mind about whatever happened to you. He felt sick when Crystal showed up like that and how she shoved everything right in your face before he had a chance to explain it to you—"

"Wait, hold on right there." I held up my hand. "You think I've moved on with Daniel?"

Alexander raised his eyebrows. "Haven't you? I mean I get it. You're both angels, so maybe that's why there's chemistry between you two, but it seems pretty obvious that you two have hooked up. You can't keep your hands off each other, although I'm a bit surprised. I thought you actually cared for Logan, but maybe we were wrong."

I hung my head, emitting an aggrieved sigh through clenched teeth.

Leveling Alexander with an icy stare, I replied, "Now *you* guys have no idea what you're talking about. The reason I'm always touching Daniel is because he keeps me from killing people!"

Xanthia raised her eyebrows, a grin spreading across her face. "Man, I wish I had a tub of popcorn right now. This shit gets better and better!"

I offered her a brief smile since it seemed like she was trying to break the tension, while Daniel stood serenely, not seeming overly perturbed by the fighting.

But unlike Daniel, I wasn't ready to let this go, not yet.

Logan's pack mates had it completely wrong, and they were accusing me of intentionally hurting Logan, when I hadn't done anything on purpose to cause him pain.

I glared at Brodie and Alexander. "Daniel is a full-blooded angel with powers just like mine, but he happens to know how to use those powers safely. And as he pointed out earlier, I'm like a brand-new angel just coming into my powers. I don't know how to use them correctly at all."

I huffed as a flush rose in my cheeks. "Apparently,

my ancestors developed a way to use our healing light only when needed. Otherwise, we kept it shoved down, but I guess that's not how we should be using it, as Daniel has informed me. So what that really means is that my entire life I've been using my light incorrectly, and now that I have this dark power back inside me, I need to relearn everything all over again. So the reason I touch Daniel, as you put it, is because his touch pushes my powers down. When I'm about to blow my lid and start shooting off red light through my hands, killing anybody within a twenty-foot radius, Daniel's power seeps into me and controls the dark power since I don't know how to do that yet."

Stepping closer, I glared up at Brodie and Alexander. "So before you go pointing fingers and accusing me of hurting Logan intentionally, maybe you should get your facts straight and start asking a few questions." I took a deep breath and tried to calm myself, but I was so pissed off that my hands shook.

Alexander raised his eyebrows, a guilty look flashing across his face. "Okay, you make a point, but with all due respect, Daria, shouldn't you take your own advice? Didn't you, just a week ago, run away from Logan without letting him explain?"

His words cut me to the quick, and my breath stopped.

Brodie shuffled his feet. "Sorry, Dar. I guess, yeah, you're right. We didn't know any of that." He peered down at me, his blue eyes back to holding their cheeky twinkle. "But damn, I don't think I've ever seen you this worked up before. I have to say, it's kinda hot."

I rolled my eyes, but my lips twitched up, then all of the anger diffused out of me. Whether that was from Daniel's touch, or the troubled expressions disappearing from Logan's pack brothers, I didn't know, but then I frowned again, remembering what Alexander had just said about me not hearing Logan out.

I nibbled my lip. He had a point.

I grimaced as guilt bit me again. "So Logan thinks that Daniel and I are together? And he thinks I've completely moved on from him and don't care about him anymore?"

Brodie sighed. "Yep. Logan thinks you viewed him as a quick fling, but for him it was . . . well . . . something else. That's why he asked us to come and escort you outta here. He couldn't handle seeing you with your *friend* anymore. I believe he said he was going to, and I quote, 'knock his fucking teeth out' if he saw Lover Boy touch you again."

My heart skipped a beat. "But I don't understand. He's still engaged to Crystal, right? So what was he doing messing around with me in the first place?"

Brodie and Alexander shared those troubled looks again.

"It's probably best if Logan tells you," Alexander replied. "It's kind of a complicated history."

Glancing at Daniel, I pulled my arm completely away from him. My powers stayed calm within me, my light locked below my navel like it always was outside of my healing sessions, and my dark . . . well, it still swirled inside me, but I didn't think I would blow anything up anytime soon.

I stepped closer to Brodie. "Can you take me to Logan? Please? I think I might have jumped to some of my own conclusions before hearing him out."

Brodie crossed his arms over his massive chest. "Are you taking Lover Boy with you? I mean, I'm not telling you what to do, especially if he keeps you from killing people, but if you want to talk to Logan, it might be best if Danny's not in the room. Logan's not exactly of rational mind right now. And if he sees you touching this guy again, he's probably gonna lose his shit."

My heart pounded. "Do you mind going back to the bus without me, Daniel? I'm sure Cecile and Mike would be happy to make up the spare bed for you."

Daniel dipped his head. "As you wish. Shall we commence your training again tomorrow after you return?"

"Yes, although I may be returning sooner than tomorrow. I'm not sure how things are going to go between Logan and me."

Daniel brushed his smooth fingers against my knuckles. "If you should need my assistance, young angel, all you need to do is call."

My eyebrows rose. "Like on a cell phone? Do you even have one of those?"

Daniel gave his coma-inducing, knee-weakening megawatt smile.

Behind me, Xanthia sighed, and even Alexander and Brodie went slack-jawed.

"No, young angel, merely call out loud for me. I shall hear you."

Daniel straightened and cleared his throat, breaking the spell he'd woven around the others, and I was glad I was immune to his angel mojo.

"I shall retreat to the *bus* for the night as you have requested, but I shall need assistance on finding the portal door from whence we came."

Alexander shook his head, his eyes clearing. "Yeah, yeah of course. No problem. Brodie, do you want to take Daria to Logan?"

Brodie raked a hand through his hair, the effects of Daniel apparently still wearing off. "Sure. Dar, you wanna follow me?"

After waving goodbye to Xanthia and Alexander before they left with Daniel, I turned on my heel and followed Brodie down the hallway toward the exterior doors. Considering where we headed, I guessed that Logan had retreated to the barracks for the night.

I hadn't been in Logan's apartment since the other night and morning in which I'd had several mind-blowing orgasms.

I shivered inwardly again when I remembered the blindfold and feather.

Brodie's nostrils flared, and he inhaled. He'd probably detected my aroused rosy scent.

My cheeks heated, but any embarrassment was cut off when I pictured another encounter with Logan. I wasn't naïve enough to think Logan would welcome me with open arms.

From the sounds of it, my werewolf ex-boyfriend was royally pissed off, and all of that anger was about to be directed at me.

Chapter 7

Cool night air washed across my cheeks when we stepped outside, but despite that soothing feeling, my palms still sweat. I rubbed them on my shorts as goose bumps pebbled my skin.

"Cold?" Brodie asked.

"Nah, I'm fine." *Just nervous.*

Moonlight pierced the night, illuminating the dark buildings ahead. The barrack's brick buildings resembled an apartment complex, standing three stories high and dotted with windows. The brick exterior mismatched the headquarters' concrete buildings behind us.

"Any words of advice?" I asked the blond werewolf when we entered the building of Logan's apartment.

Brodie scratched his chin as the door shut behind us. "Just hear him out. If he's talking to you, that is." He winked.

"Ha-ha."

We rounded the corner to Logan's hallway. When we got to his door, I paused. *Here goes nothing.*

I was about to raise my hand to knock when Brodie stepped in front of me, his broad shoulders cutting off my view.

"It's probably best if you just go in. I'm not sure if he'll answer a knock." Brodie laid his finger across the holograph lock above the door handle. It clicked.

He pushed the door open before I had a chance to collect my thoughts then pushed me inside when the door was wide enough for me to slip through.

"Good luck," he whispered and closed the door behind me, engaging the lock again.

The soft click sounded like a death sentence.

Turning around to face whatever was to come, I squinted. Logan's apartment was dimly lit but looked exactly as I remembered it. Off to the right lay a large living room with two couches, a few tables, a standing lamp, and a TV hanging on the wall. On the left stood a counter with stools that overlooked the open kitchen.

Only a single lamp illuminated the open design.

"Logan?" I called, stepping forward after slipping my shoes off. My feet sank into the thick carpet.

I looked around for him, my footsteps silent, but he wasn't in the kitchen, the living room, or the bathroom. That only left one option.

The bedroom.

A closed door greeted me when I slid my hand

around the cool metallic door handle. Before I lost my nerve, I twisted it and pushed the door open.

A dark bedroom greeted me, and standing directly in front of the window, looking out at the shadowed distant mountains, stood Logan. His back was to me, his hands stuffed into his pockets.

I stepped into the room, my breath catching in my throat.

"You've decided to speak with me after all?" His voice came out hoarse, but he didn't turn.

"Maybe." I closed the door quietly behind me.

"Is he with you? Your new boyfriend? I can't smell him, so does that mean he's in the hall?"

I laced my fingers together. Already, I wanted to fidget. "No. I'm alone."

He raked a hand through his hair, agitated energy growing off him. "But you're going back to him tonight?"

I took another hesitant step forward. "I'm not with him."

Logan swung around. Deep-gold light illuminated his eyes. "But you've slept with him?" Intense pain lined his face.

"No." I took a deep breath and added quietly, "But shouldn't you be the one answering my questions? You lied to me about Crystal. You said you didn't have a girlfriend."

Logan looked down, his chest rising and falling rapidly with each short breath. "I know. I fucked up. Trust me, I know, and I've been kicking myself ever since you ran away." He raised his head, that deep groove between his eyes. "So you're really telling me you've been with Daniel for a week and haven't hooked up with him?"

I cocked my head, wondering if he would truly lose all interest in me if I had. Logan had made quite a big deal out of me being a virgin. If I wasn't anymore, maybe he wouldn't want me at all. "And what if I had? Would you tell me to leave? Because I wouldn't be a prized virgin anymore?"

His head snapped back. Anguish distorted his features. "No. It's not like that. I just need to know if he's touched you. I wouldn't . . ." He swallowed audibly, his jaw hardening. "I wouldn't hold it against you. I would still want you, but I *need* to know."

I scoffed. "You wouldn't hold it against me?"

He took a step closer to me. "Please, Dar. Just put me out of my fucking misery and tell me if you've fucked him."

I sighed, knowing he wasn't going to let it go until I answered. "No. Okay? He hasn't touched me. It's not like that. You're still the only one I've been with like that."

Logan's fists, which had been balled at his sides, relaxed. "So you haven't slept with him? Even though you and him keep touching?"

"For goodness' sake, Logan. No! How many times do I need to say it? Daniel and I are friends. I met him when I stepped through an angel portal back in the supernatural marketplace, and I was transported to Emunda. He's taken pity on me and has agreed to train me so I can learn how to control this freakin' dark power inside me." As if aware that I'd spoken of it, the dark power shifted in my belly, beckoning me to let it loose.

"Angel portal?" Logan's eyebrows rose. "Emunda?"

But I ignored his shocked expression and crossed my arms. "And what about you? Did you sleep with Crystal while I was gone?" I held my breath, *hating* how much the thought of Logan with Crystal hurt me.

A look of disbelief washed over Logan's face. "No, of course not. I'm with you."

With me? What kind of fucked-up world did Logan live in if he considered himself with me while engaged to someone else?

"What about before I met you? You must have slept with her then. How long have you been fucking *her?*" Jealousy coursed through me, sparking the dark power even more.

"I haven't."

"You haven't slept with her?" My eyebrows rose. "Not ever?"

"No. Not ever."

My crossed arms fell and dangled listlessly at my sides. "You're really telling me that you haven't slept with your fiancée?" My tone dripped with skepticism.

He dipped his head again. "She's been my intended wife since we were little kids, but I've never been with her. I've had brief relationships and hookups throughout the years, like most guys my age, but I've never slept with Crystal. She's my fiancée on paper only. That's why I said I didn't have a girlfriend, because in my mind, I don't. Crystal doesn't mean anything to me. She never has."

My knees collapsed beneath me, and I sank onto

Logan's bed. "I don't understand. She was all over you at the marketplace, and she seemed intent on letting me know that you were hers, and that text I saw back on my tour..."

I'd let Logan know that I'd seen a text Crystal sent him, back when he'd been my bodyguard only. The words from that text had been branded in my mind, like a tattoo I couldn't erase. It was that text that had led me to believe he had a girlfriend.

"... *miss you. When can you call? I've been...*"

Logan shook his head. "We talk occasionally, and she's always trying to act like we're more than what we are, although lately, she's been a bit weird. But sometimes I reply to her messages. Other times I don't. But no matter what she says, I keep my responses formal and polite. I've never tried to lead her to believe that I feel more than what I do."

"Well, she could have fooled me with how she was acting at the marketplace."

"She's met a few of my flings previously—"

"Like Holly?"

"Holly?" A stumped expression covered his face.

"You know, the red-haired cloaking witch who was all over you after Jayden attacked me?"

"I never dated Holly."

"Oh, you haven't? I just assumed you'd been with her."

"No, Holly acts like that because I keep rejecting her, but forget about Holly. Who gives a shit about Holly?"

Okay, then. Apparently, not Logan. But despite his harsh

words, relief poured through me.

Logan came closer to the other side of the bed. "But back to Crystal. She knows you're different. Rumors about you have spread in my pack, and people are talking. I think that's why she's gotten worked up, cause before, she's always successfully run off other women I've been with. But with those women, I didn't care. They were a distraction more than anything, but with you . . ." His voice turned hoarse, the gold in his eyes brightening again. "You're different, and she knows it. I won't let her run you off, and she feels threatened by that. I've never wanted anyone like I want you, and she's worried you're going to take her place as my future wife."

For a moment, my breath stopped. Did he just say his *future wife?* Anticipation prickled my skin.

"So . . . what you and Crystal have is like . . . an arranged marriage or something?"

"Basically, yeah."

"And there's no way out of it?"

He hung his head and raked a hand through his hair then sat on the other side of his bed, the mattress sinking in his direction. Since he was so close, his scent fluttered to me, the sandalwood fragrance I loved so much.

Acutely aware of how closely he sat, my nerves tingled. I wanted to reach for him, to touch him, but I couldn't. Even if everything had been fine between us, the dark power still resided inside me. Until Daniel taught me how to control it, things were as frustratingly unresolved as they'd been the previous week.

"It's complicated," he finally replied.

"Then help me understand." I scooted closer to him, still careful to maintain a safe distance.

He put his hand on the bed, his fingers only inches from mine. "As you know, I'm supposed to be the alpha of my pack one day. This stint with the SF is supposed to be short-term only. My real responsibility lies at home. Since I'm the future alpha, there are certain expectations for me. I'm supposed to marry the highest-ranking female of a rival pack, which is Crystal. She's the only daughter of her pack's alpha, and as the only female born to any rival alpha, she was the only option for me."

"Okay. I'm following you so far."

"As I told you before, there are three packs in the US—my pack in Wyoming, the Montana pack, and the Idaho pack. Crystal's from the Idaho pack. The Montana pack's alpha only had sons, so there weren't any females from that pack to choose from. Crystal was literally the only choice, and my parents fought hard for me to get her. That's part of the problem. The Montana pack's alpha wanted her for his son, too, so it came down to a challenge. I was too young to remember it, but my dad challenged the Montana alpha. From what I've been told, the match was bloody, and both of them nearly died, but it was that match that solidified my betrothal to Crystal. So if I back out of the arranged marriage now, I'll be completely dishonoring my family. My parents would be heartbroken, and Crystal's pack would insist on war with our pack. And alphas always marry other female werewolves. It's always been that way." His chin dipped. "Tradition in the werewolf world means everything."

I nibbled my lip then sat up straighter. "But you have a brother, right? Why can't he be alpha and you step down?"

"It doesn't work that way. The oldest is first in line to be alpha. Always. The only way around that is if a younger brother is more dominant."

I slumped. "And I'm guessing Lucas isn't as dominant?"

"No. If he were, my life would be much easier. He could marry Crystal and be alpha. I'd be free to live as I pleased."

When he finished, I just sat there.

Everything he'd told me sounded so foreign. I had no understanding of the werewolf world. Hell, my entire life, I hadn't even *known* there were werewolves. I pulled my hand into my lap, even though I wanted to grasp his and tell him we would find a way, but suddenly . . .

I didn't know if we would.

"So that's who Crystal is." His jaw clenched again, and for the first time, I *really* saw how heavily his responsibilities weighed on him.

"Where is she now?"

"Either back in Hidden Creek, my hometown, or her hometown in Idaho. There's a lot going on with our betrothal right now. I'm surprised she was able to get down here at all, but at least I don't think she intends on coming back to Boise anytime soon. You don't need to worry about her sneaking up on us again." But that weighted look stayed in his eyes before he veiled it, forcing a smile. "Now, are you going to tell me what you've been doing for the past week? And who this Daniel guy is? When you disappeared in that shop in the marketplace, where did you go?"

Though I tried to smile, it fell short. "I didn't know I'd be gone for a week after I stepped through that portal. A week here felt like a few hours in Emunda."

"Emunda? Is that where the vendor's portal took you?"

I told him everything—how I'd seen the psychic that I'd first met when I was a teenager while Logan and I were shopping; how she'd told me to visit Vendor 109; how I'd dashed into the angel portal in the back of Vendor 109's shop; how I'd been transported to the realm for lost angels; and how Daniel had found me there and offered to train me in hopes it would find him in our maker's good graces again.

"It's possible to exist with both my dark and light, according to Daniel. And apparently, the way I've been controlling my light is entirely wrong. He said I'm like a baby angel, completely untrained. I have to be taught all over again, like when my mom taught me as a child."

Logan listened intently, that subtle glow still in his eyes.

I went on to explain what Master Gregor had revealed about my distant grandfather being an archangel and how it was his blood—not Dillon Parker's blood—that flowed through my veins, and about how my family had been forced to become executioners.

"Executioners?" Logan's head snapped back.

"It was around that time that the Gresham women

disappeared, and my guess is that's also when we excommunicated ourselves from the community. I think my family went into hiding to protect themselves and future generations from further manipulations."

"Because your ancestors knew if powerful rulers found them again, their powers could be used to kill once more."

"Exactly," I replied.

I shifted back to lean against the headboard. The clock read after eleven, yet I was anything but tired. It was hard to believe I'd already been at Logan's apartment for over an hour. "But I still don't know how my ancestors got rid of their dark power. That still remains a mystery."

"Do you think there's a way to find out?" Logan stretched out, his long, hard form taking up half the bed. He lay on his side, his head cupped in his hand.

I tried to ignore his chest muscles pressed against his thin shirt and the distinctive bulge in his pants. I remembered his size all too well from when he'd been naked right next to me, very similar to how we lay at the moment.

Snapping my gaze away, I said, "Maybe. Master Gregor is going to do some more searching."

He rested back against the bed, his alert gaze sliding up and down my frame. "So why were you able to touch me when you only had your light, but you can't with your dark? If your dark power was always a part of you, shouldn't it act like your light and not respond to potential mates?"

I shrugged. "You would think so. I asked Daniel the

same thing, and he said that he's unfamiliar with the tactics my family developed to control our powers, but he's guessing it's because this power is new to me, so I'm completely overwhelmed by it, whereas my light is something I've felt since I was a small child."

"Makes sense, I guess."

"Yep, but it doesn't make this any easier." I waved at the two feet of distance between us.

He sighed heavily, grim acceptance filling his eyes. "Do you know that Emunda isn't something supernaturals are aware of? And that explains why that Victor guy was so agitated every time I showed up. He must be commissioned by the angels to guard that portal. I have a feeling the SF will be monitoring Victor's shop very closely from now on. We don't like unknown portals."

"Yeah, Daniel said Emunda portals are rare."

A moment of silence fell.

Logan threaded his strong, lean fingers through his dark hair, making me itch to touch him. I distinctly remembered how those hands felt gliding along my skin at that hill above the rest stop, and how he'd used those hands to drape a feather across my body and rub other things against me which had given me the most intense orgasm of my life.

I rearranged how I was sitting, my core swelling with desire.

Logan's eyelids dipped, his voice growing husky. "You're giving off that scent again."

I laughed humorlessly. "What scent? The roses-in-heat one?"

He inched closer. "That's the one." He inhaled deeply. "You have no idea what that smell does to me."

I squirmed—which was a mistake. The friction against my core, Logan's heat warming me, and his intoxicating scent all worked against me.

"Your scent does things to me too." I groaned in frustration. "Maybe I should go."

"Don't." He reached for me but let his hand drop at the last second. His large fingers fell back onto the bed.

I ached to touch him. Ached so much it actually hurt. "I still can't control my dark power. I don't want to hurt you."

"You won't."

"You don't know that."

"You're right, I don't. But you haven't hurt me yet."

"That's probably sheer luck. You should have seen me in my first training session this morning. Every time I tried to let my powers flow under my skin like Daniel instructed, energy burst from me. It knocked me off my feet a few times."

"So you're supposed to let them be free? Together?"

I nodded, the movement making my long blond hair brush around my shoulders. I swiped it aside but not before I saw how prominently my nipples pressed against my shirt.

Logan's gaze darkened when he saw my breasts swelling. "Damn, woman." He shook himself, abruptly looking away and clearing his throat. "Okay, tell me more about what Daniel's told you."

I explained how Daniel had said full-blooded angels lived with both of their powers together, and how angelic light was created for healing people and the dark power was for banishing evil.

"So you need to let your dark power be like your light when you're around me," Logan said after I finished.

I cocked my head. "What do you mean?"

"With me, your light stayed calm, right? And isn't that how it's *always* supposed to be with everyone according to Daniel? Even when you're not around a potential mate? So you need to let your dark power do the same. Let it flow freely, even when I touch you."

"But what if I can't and I hurt you?"

Logan gave a crooked smile. "I'm pretty quick on my feet. I'll move out of the way in time." He inched closer.

My insides immediately seized up, like someone had trapped me in a vise. Never mind that Logan was still engaged. I had no idea how he and I could ever be together, but I still wanted him as much as he wanted me.

That's a problem for another day.

"Logan . . ." My tone turned low and warning. The dark power swirled, a jolt of panic shooting through me.

"Just relax." His calm, deep voice didn't waver despite me going ramrod still. "Close your eyes. Try to focus on what Daniel told you. Let your powers mix. Don't separate them so much."

Taking a deep breath, I did as he said and closed my eyes.

The bed dipped, letting me know Logan had shifted even closer. A brush of fabric—his jeans—tickled the back of my hand.

"That's it. Just take deep breaths, nice and slow."

I concentrated on my breathing and the soothing cadence of his deep voice. The bed dipped more, warmth seeping into my skin, but I was too scared to open my eyes. I was too scared to see Logan so close. I squeezed my eyes more tightly shut.

"Relax. Just breathe." His breath puffed against my neck.

Goose bumps rose on my arms, and a delicious tingle ran down my spine. I turned inward even more, feeling my powers below my navel. They swirled, both there, both present, but the dark tried to rise again, pushing above my light, like a neglected child who wanted all of the attention.

"I can't," I said through clenched teeth. I pushed my powers back down, my entire body stiffening.

"You're doing fine. Try again when you're ready."

The strength of Logan's voice, his absolute conviction that I could learn to master my angel powers, helped slow my pounding heart. I took another deep breath, feeling inside for my powers again.

That time, when I cracked the well where my healing light lived, I did it without hesitation. I wrenched it open, but I had faith that Logan could indeed get out of the way if he needed to.

My light flowed upward, zapping my skin and filling my body. The dark power moved hot on its tail, clenching and attacking my limbs like a rabid dog that bit everything in its path.

But instead of panicking and shoving it back down as fast as I could, I concentrated more on my breath, taking deep inhalations.

My dark power jolted down my arms, moving faster and more efficiently than my light. When it reached my hands, I tensed. "Logan, it's going—"

"It's all right." His calm words flowed toward me. "You've got this. Let it go."

I sank into the pillow as my dark and light powers, for the very first time, intermixed. I gasped. Radiant, bold energy spun through my body, heightening the feel of every pore, saturating every cell. A smile parted my lips as an incredible sense of power flowed along my skin.

"You have no idea how beautiful you are right now." Logan's breath puffed against my lips, and then—

His lips were on mine, tasting my skin as his tongue flicked across my bottom lip. I gasped again, my eyes still closed.

"Logan," I said breathlessly, reaching for him, needing him and wanting him more than I ever had before.

"Yeah, babe. I'm right here." His hand settled onto my hip, drawing my body flush against his. The brush of his clothes, the taste of his tongue, and the warmth of his hand were like thousands of rays of sunshine bursting into my soul.

I felt alive.

Powerful.

And aroused as hell.

"Your scent just got a hundred times stronger." He

growled and nipped at my neck, his teeth grazing against the sensitive skin near my ear. His hand slid under my shirt, caressing my back and sending shooting tingles to my toes.

"Ahh!" I arched up as jolts of electricity zinged down my abdomen, my core clenching with liquid heat.

"Fuck, it feels good to touch you again." He growled softly against my neck before dipping his hand into the waistband of my shorts and cupping my ass. He kneaded the soft flesh, another possessive growl coming from his throat.

I grabbed onto him. My breasts strained against my shirt, begging to be let free as he hooked my leg around his waist. I ran my hands up and down his back, around his shoulders, and down his waist. Every inch of him felt hot and hard. *So hard.* His erection throbbed against my abdomen. I longed to feel his length, and my fingers fumbled with his zipper.

"Yeah, touch me, babe. God, I've missed you." He claimed my mouth again, his firm lips molding to mine.

We kissed for I didn't know how long as my fingers dipped into his pants and ran up and down his steel length. He groaned and pulled back, pressing urgent kisses down my neck.

My skin felt on fire for him. Every inch of me was so hot. My angel powers continued to flow through me, buzzing and vibrating.

All of it was so much. My powers. Logan. Our bodies. Everything.

"I need . . ." I struggled to find the words, my eyes

still closed. "I want . . ."

"I know what you want." He reached around and cupped my mound between my legs, his finger tickling my most sensitive area.

I cried out again, my body bucking wildly against his. "Logan!" When I opened my eyes, his dark hooded gaze was only inches from mine. A soft smile curved my lips. "We're touching again, babe."

I smiled, a grin stretching across my face as my desire increased exponentially.

And then—

My dark and light powers burst from my limbs in an uncontrolled cataclysm of energy.

"No!" I yelled as a mixture of desire, frustration, and pent-up need exploded from my body. Red and gold light shot from my chest and limbs like meteors blazing across the sky.

My power exploded into Logan.

He flew across the room and smashed into the wall before crumbling to the floor. His entire body lay terrifyingly still.

I screamed, scrambling from the bed, panic making my limbs clumsy and uncontrolled. "Logan!"

But then I saw my glowing skin. I dove away, using Logan's bed to shield him from my powers.

Wood splintered, covers shredded, and drywall cracked as my angel powers wreaked havoc on his room. Red and gold light continued to pour from me in uncontrolled blasts, my angel powers entirely unleashed.

I tried my hardest to control my powers, stuff them

down, push them into oblivion, but my body turned into an exploding inferno.

"No! No! No!" I searched frantically for a phone, or a magical button, or *something* to get help.

But there was nothing.

Absolutely nothing.

Closing my eyes, I leaned my head back and yelled, "Daniel! I need you!"

Chapter 8

Daniel was in the room before I blinked, materializing from thin air. "You require my assistance, young angel?"

I'd sunk against the wall, my powers cracking the drywall as my heart thumped a thousand miles an hour. "Help me! Oh my god, I killed him! I think I killed him!"

Explosions of red and gold light continued to shoot from my body. I curled in on myself, trying to stop it, but I could only contain it so much.

Every time the red shot from my fingertips, whatever was in its path blew up. A lamp shattered. A picture shot from the wall. A corner of the dresser's top splintered.

In two strides, Daniel was at my side, his hands settling on my shoulders.

And just like that, my explosions stopped.

Daniel's soothing power rushed into me, intermingling with my dark and light. My light slithered back into the storage chest below my navel, while my dark power slunk back into my belly. He continued to touch me, eyes closed, as a serene expression covered his face.

Once my light was fully contained in my internal storage chest, I slammed the cover down as my dark coiled in on itself like a snake that could once again strike.

Daniel let go of my shoulders, but I grabbed his hand, sobbing, not trusting myself to keep my dark power there. Panic made it hard to breathe.

"I think I killed him! I think Logan's dead!"

Expecting to see a horrified expression on Daniel's face, my mouth fell open when I saw him grinning.

"Your strength is quite admirable for an angel that is only a half-breed."

A sob choked me, then another. "Didn't you hear me?" I rushed to Logan's side, pulling Daniel with me. "Forget about my power's strength. Help him!"

"Shush, young angel." Daniel calmly kneeled by Logan's chest while still holding my hand. "Logan is fine, merely knocked unconscious. See? He breathes evenly and deeply."

My petrified gaze slid along Logan's still form. Some of the adrenaline spiking through my veins slowed.

Daniel was right. Logan was still breathing.

"But what if he's injured? What if he has head trauma or internal bleeding?"

"Then we shall heal him." Daniel placed my hands on

Logan's chest. "Use your power. Feel for any injuries."

"I can't! I can't!" I snatched my hands away from Logan.

"You *can*. You underestimate yourself. You're very strong, young angel, stronger than I anticipated. Harness that strength. Use it as our maker intended you to."

"But what if I hurt him more?"

"You won't."

I scoffed and ran an agitated hand through my hair. Already, my dark power was uncoiling, threatening to rise again. "That's what Logan said, that I wouldn't hurt him, and look what happened."

"You were practicing without me?" An intrigued sparkle lit his eyes.

My cheeks heated, remembering Logan's lips on mine. "Um, kind of."

"Well, never mind about all of that. Now . . ." He took my hands again and placed them over Logan's chest. "Heal him."

I sighed. "Okay. I'll try."

I kept my thigh pressed against Daniel's knee. Closing my eyes, I carefully lifted the lid on my healing light. The dark power stirred, as if knowing I was calling upon my light, but with Daniel's help, I kept it in check.

Taking a deep breath, I searched Logan's body for injuries, exactly as I would have in a healing session with my clients.

"No, young angel. Don't detach your light from yourself to search Logan's body with your power. You and your powers are one."

I opened my eyes, groaning in frustration. "But I don't know how to do that."

"Yes, you do. You're fighting it."

The only thing that kept me from screaming was knowing that Logan wasn't seriously injured. If he had been, I was fairly certain Daniel would have jumped in and healed him.

"Fine. I'll try again." I placed my hands above Logan's chest, his steady inhalations and exhalations alleviating some of my panic. *Here goes nothing.*

Opening the chest once again, I did exactly what I had done before when Logan and I had been fooling around. I let it blow wide-open and didn't stop my light when it rushed forward, my dark hot on its tail.

"That's it." Daniel's approval penetrated my senses, but I didn't pay him any attention. It was requiring all of my concentration not to become a human firework again.

Similar to when Logan and I had been on his bed, my powers rushed along my limbs, my light underneath my skin, setting my nerves on fire while the cold dark power followed, dousing my light's flame. That same rush of power and awareness coursed through me.

"Much better, Daria. You look like a beautiful angel right now. Your skin is glowing."

Remembering Logan saying something about how I'd looked beautiful at that stage, I tentatively opened my eyes.

I gasped.

My bare arms and legs indeed glowed. A subtle hue floated around my body, like sparkly light hovering over my entire being.

"I do look like an angel." I flipped my hands back and forth, marveling at the power coursing through me. But at the same time, I knew that was because Daniel and I still shared contact. "But how do I look normal so I don't stand out in the human world?"

"You temper it, but we'll get to that. Now, heal him." Daniel's patient yet insistent tone let me know that he wasn't going to help.

I placed my hands above Logan's chest again. "Do I do this like a healing session?"

"Since I have never seen you heal before, I am not sure, but do what feels natural to you. I want to see how you have previously healed."

Feeling a little more confident, I settled in at Logan's side. I'd done more healings than I could count, and instinct took over.

I shifted and swayed, letting my light run over Logan's body. Amazingly, my dark power swayed with it but didn't attack. I again felt fairly certain that was because Daniel still touched me.

"I can't believe it," I whispered.

Daniel had been right. Despite the tremendous force my red light had dealt Logan, he wasn't overly harmed. The only injury I could find was a slight concussion, which no doubt explained the unconsciousness. "No broken bones. No internal bleeding. No bruised organs. It's amazing. That blast would have killed a human."

Daniel chuckled. "Werewolves are not easy to kill, in case you were unaware of that fact."

"That's probably good. I'm not sure another species could handle me."

My hands grew hot as I returned my attention to healing. Weaving my light into Logan's body, I slithered it up his spinal column into his mind. Encompassing his brain, I healed the small injury I found there.

Just as I finished, his eyes opened.

"Daria?" His deep voice carried to me like a breeze on a humid summer night.

"Logan!" I sucked my power back inside me, falling back into my old habits as I stuffed my light into the chest. The dark power rolled.

Daniel *tsked*, but I didn't pay him any attention.

I flung my arms around Logan, burying my face in his neck.

"Are you okay, babe?"

His concern only made me sob more. "I thought I killed you."

He laughed, a deep rumble in his chest. "I told you that you wouldn't hurt me."

"But I did!" I pulled back just enough to let him sit up. "You flew off the bed and smashed into the wall. I gave you a concussion, but I just healed your brain, so you should be fine."

Logan felt the back of his head. "You healed me?"

I glanced at Daniel discreetly before meeting Logan's gaze again. "I had help."

Logan shifted his attention to Daniel, an edge entering his tone. "I thought you said you came here alone."

"I did. I wasn't lying. Daniel came after I called him for help." I left out how the angel had materialized from thin air.

Logan cleared his throat and grunted. "I guess I should thank you then."

Daniel dipped his head. "It was my pleasure."

I wrapped my arms around Logan again and started to rise. "Let me help you up."

But Logan stayed firmly planted on the ground.

He withdrew my hands from around his chest and, for a moment, just stared at them. "I'm touching you right now, and you're not concentrating. How is that possible?"

I nodded in Daniel's direction. "He's keeping me from killing anybody."

He looked at where Daniel's and my feet were touching, and his brow furrowed. "Well, that's awkward."

I laughed. "Hopefully, it's only temporary. Daniel said I just need to learn how to exist with my powers and then I won't need him anymore."

"Daria has much strength, but as I'm coming to learn, she often underestimates herself. She's made remarkable progress in the short time I've worked with her."

Pride gleamed in Logan's eyes. "I always knew she was a fast learner." He stood but wouldn't let me help him. "I'm fine, Dar. Seriously, don't worry about me. This is nothing compared to some injuries I've had."

I winced, remembering the dangerous work he did for the SF. I wasn't sure if I wanted to know about the previous injuries or not.

Logan grazed his knuckles across my cheeks, his eyes softening. "It feels so good to touch you again."

Acutely aware of Daniel standing right beside us, my cheeks heated. In typical fashion, the angel seemed completely oblivious to human customs. Instead of turning his back, and giving Logan and me privacy, Daniel continued to hover over us, watching our entire interaction.

"It's . . . uh . . . getting late." I cleared my throat. "I suppose we should all turn in."

"Do you need any further assistance, young angel?" Daniel asked.

"No, I think I'm done experimenting with my powers for the night. Thank you for coming."

Logan seemed reluctant to let our contact break, but with a curt nod, he stepped back, dropping his hand.

I missed his touch immediately. The brush from his knuckles tingled along my cheek. I resisted the urge to reach up and touch my skin.

"Are you staying here?" Logan asked in a husky voice.

I shook my head vigorously. "No. I don't want to hurt you again. It's probably best if I go back to the bus for tonight."

Logan's eyes dimmed. "I'll see you tomorrow?"

"Yeah. I'd like that."

As if finally reassured that things between us were back on track, even though he was still engaged, Logan smiled.

My knees grew weak at the sight. *Damn.* There was something about Logan Smith that completely took my breath away.

He stepped closer, leaning in, his nostrils flaring. "There's that smell again."

I playfully smacked him but then stopped the second I did. I wasn't touching Daniel at the moment.

My eyes widened with horror. I waited for my powers to come bursting forth from their depths. A second ticked by, then another, and my shoulders began to relax. My powers hadn't responded that time.

"You're already making progress, young angel." Daniel clasped his hands behind his back.

For the first time since the dark power had been born inside me, I felt a sense of hope. "You're right. In that moment, they didn't grow out of control."

Logan smiled, his lips curving up in that delicious way that made me want to plant my mouth on his. I hastily took another breath before my arousal grew completely out of control.

"So what's the plan for tomorrow?" Logan crossed his arms over his chest, his huge biceps flexing as he took in his destroyed room.

"Daniel and I planned to train again in the morning." I eyed the cracked walls and broken furniture. "I'm sorry about all of this."

Logan shrugged. "Don't be. I'll call Sephera in. She specializes in reconstructive spells. It shouldn't take her more than five minutes to fix this."

I breathed a sigh of relief.

Logan rubbed the stubble on his chin. "Anyway, I'll have to report to work in the morning, but I can meet up with you in the afternoon."

I nibbled on my lower lip. Despite the future still being so unsure and Crystal's presence looming in the back of my mind, I knew that at the moment, our situation was what it was and couldn't be changed.

Either I accepted that, or I didn't.

But I already knew my decision. I wanted Logan. I had from the moment I'd laid eyes on him, and he'd made it clear he wanted me too.

All of our other troubles would eventually resurface, and it was possible we wouldn't be together in the future, but at the moment, we could be.

I smiled. "Yeah, I would like that."

Chapter 9

Over the next few weeks, I trained daily with Daniel. Each day, I thought of my clients, the sick people I'd left behind with promises to heal them once I returned to work. But unless I successfully learned how to live with my angel powers, I would never be able to help them.

That motivation helped, pushing me to train long hours each day.

Unfortunately, those sessions usually went similarly to how my first day with Daniel had gone, but sometimes, they didn't. On some days, my powers would flow together, my body glowing like a dim star, and I would feel that immense power again as I harnessed my full potential.

But a lot of times, that wasn't what happened.

"Ahh!" I screamed as I launched into the air, red light bursting from my body.

It was my third acrobatic disaster that morning. Wind sailed across my cheeks, and my muscles flexed at the coming impact. The ground grew closer.

"Ugh!" I landed hard, and once again . . . in the mud.

I pushed up, staring at my ruined pants as agony ripped through my body. "Seriously?"

It was the second time I'd managed to land in the field's only mud pile. Dark stains marred my jeans, and dirt caked under my fingernails. With a huff, I brushed my hair back. I was pretty sure my escaped hair resembled a bird's nest.

"I'm never going to get the hang of this," I grumbled.

Daniel strolled to my side, his white pants and shirt pristine. Even in the dirty meadow, he managed to stay impeccable. "You're doing wonderfully, young angel. Four times already this morning, you managed to call forth your power without it bursting from your body." He gave me a sympathetic smile. "Of course, not this last one, but still, you are making progress."

I sighed. "If you say so."

Daniel gave me a hand up. "Now, let's begin again."

"I was afraid of that." I readied myself for another nasty encounter with my powers. In between each session, I locked my light back inside the chest within my belly while my dark waited impatiently free.

I still didn't know how to get rid of that safe haven for my light. It was something I had lived with my entire life, so to try to obliterate it completely made me panic.

"We'll get there," Daniel said, his uncanny sense into people's emotions making itself known again, before he moved a few feet away.

I dusted off my pants. A cool nip hung in the air, which was why I'd opted to wear jeans. I was about to ask how much longer we had to train for the day when the hairs on the back of my neck stood on end.

Someone was watching us.

I twirled around as Daniel's perfect eyebrows rose. "Is something amiss, young angel?"

"Are we being watched?"

Daniel merely nodded, not looking the least bit perturbed. "He's been there for a while." He subtly inclined his head toward the trees.

My eyes narrowed as I searched for our audience. After a quick scan, I spotted him. A tall, middle-aged man stood in the trees, partially hidden by a large aspen. He wore a long coat and sunglasses, but I still felt his interest, which seemed to pulse from him in steady waves.

I took a step toward him, but as soon as he realized that I'd spotted him, he turned and fled through the trees.

"What the heck," I muttered. "Who was he?"

Daniel shrugged. "A curious observer, perhaps?"

I didn't explain to my angel friend that a supernatural hiding in the woods, watching me train was a little odd. But then I remembered how I had celebrity status in the supernatural world.

Perhaps my angel power training was no longer a secret and I'd garnered a few curious onlookers.

Brushing it off, I asked Daniel, "Say, I've been

meaning to ask you—can you teach me how to move from place to place and materialize in thin air?"

Daniel placed his large hands with his elegant fingers on his hips. "Are you speaking of teleportation?" A look of genuine regret filled his face. "I'm afraid not, young angel. You must be full-blooded to govern that power."

"Oh. Bummer."

His lips quirked up. "Now, close your eyes. For whatever reason, I have the distinct impression that you're stalling."

"Maybe it's because my butt's sore, and I don't really feel like landing on it again."

Daniel chuckled then smoothed his expression. "Begin. Open your powers. Banish that chest that you store your light in. Become one with your dark and light."

I did as he said, once again calling forth both of my powers. The chest opened, and my light rushed forward but not as quickly as it had during my last attempt. And my dark didn't feel like it was trying to dominate my light quite as much.

While a part of me knew that Daniel was right and I was making progress, that progress was still extremely slow.

We carried on for another few hours. By the time we finished, my body hurt everywhere. It wasn't just from the multiple landings or the bursts of energy from my body, but it was mental exhaustion too.

Undoing all of the bad habits I had learned throughout my life was proving to be more challenging than I'd anticipated. In a way, it felt as if my mind had run a marathon.

When we finished, I bent over, hands on my knees, and panted. Faint clapping reached my ears.

I straightened and twirled around, searching for the source, half expecting to see that same guy who'd been watching me earlier.

Instead, my heart jumped into my throat when I spotted Logan leaning against a tree at the edge of the field. His broad shoulders brushed on its trunk while he clapped his hands.

Giddiness rose inside me. We'd seen each other every day since I'd returned from Emunda, but we hadn't risked another make-out session. Despite the intense physical chemistry Logan and I shared, I wasn't willing to risk another sensual encounter with him. The stakes were too high.

The one night we had, when Daniel had rescued me, had been lucky. None of Logan's neighbors had been injured even though their drywall had cracked too. Thankfully, Sephera had repaired all of it.

Bottom line, I needed to learn how to live with my powers first.

I jogged to Logan's side, ignoring my protesting muscles as the field's tall grass brushed against my thighs.

"Hi." The word came out breathless when I finally reached him.

Logan's eyelids grew hooded. "Hi to you. I have to say, that was pretty impressive."

I tucked another strand of hair behind my ear and grimaced. "I'm not sure if I agree with you." I waved at my mud-stained pants. "Daniel's a good coach, but I'm not the best student."

Logan pushed away from the tree. "Don't say that. You're doing great. Twice, you had that glowing hue around your body, which means you're making progress, and once you master your powers, I can touch you again." His voice dipped. "In all the places I keep dreaming about."

Desire flamed in my core. "Well, if that's not motivation, I don't know what is."

He laughed, the sound rich and deep. My belly clenched, and the familiar longing to touch him returned.

Footsteps swished through the grass behind us. A quick glance over my shoulder revealed Daniel approaching.

Clearing my throat, I tried to wrangle my hormones back under control before asking Logan, "How was work this morning?"

Logan's jaw locked, his soft expression vanishing as a grim one took its place. "Not good. There was another attack last night."

My jaw dropped. "Another one? Was anybody hurt?" That was the fifth attack in the last two weeks.

"Unfortunately, yeah. Four SF members were injured."

"*Another* attack on the SF?" My uneasiness grew.

Daniel reached my side, the subtle brush of his arm against mine alerting me to his presence, but my attention stayed focused on Logan. "What happened?"

"A squad of six SF members was patrolling a New

York City suburb for a nest of particularly nasty vampires. We've been pursuing them for months but haven't been able to trap them. But last night, it seems they lured the SF members to them. What the squad thought was a warehouse fronting as the vampires' business turned out to be an ambush zone. Similar to that attack in Arkansas last week, each vampire that attacked had red eyes."

"Did you know they had red eyes? Is that why you'd been following them?"

Logan shook his head. "That's the strange part. During the past few months, we've taken multiple pictures of them and have acquired numerous hours of security footage, but in none of that footage does it show red eyes in any of them. Why they looked that way last night is still something we can't explain."

I shivered. "Do you have any idea what all of this means?"

"At this point, it's fairly obvious. The Supernatural Forces are under a covert attack, but from what, we don't know, and since they strike randomly, it's very hard to anticipate when the next one will be."

Goose bumps erupted on my forearms. I rubbed them, wrapping my arms closely around my middle. Logan was right. Other than my attack, and a few others, *all* of the red-eyed attacks had been against SF members.

A memory of the attack I'd suffered only weeks before by three red-eyed rogue werewolves brushed the back of my mind. Jayden had made a comment during the attack, about how someone named S wanted them hunting someone in particular.

Perhaps SF members?

I nibbled on my fingertip. "Has there been anything found about S?"

Logan's expression grew grimmer. "We're only twenty percent through the list of supernaturals with a name starting with S. So to answer your question, no."

"And you're sure no attacks like this have ever happened before? Even hundreds of years ago?"

"Not that we're aware of, but Master Gregor is on it. Wes got unlimited time from the courts this morning. Everyone is taking this threat seriously."

My stomach churned, and I nodded in agreement. "It's definitely best that *all* of Master Gregor's time is spent studying that."

Logan stepped closer, his hand lifting, as if he wanted to brush a finger across my cheek. At the last moment, he stopped. "We'll still search for answers about your family. Master Gregor's no longer being at your disposal doesn't mean we'll stop searching."

"At least I know what I am now and more about the women in my family. A few weeks ago, I didn't know any of that." I turned to Daniel. "Do you know anything about supernaturals with red eyes?"

The angel stood calmly in the late-morning sun, his arms hanging listlessly at his sides. With the sun shining over his shoulders, he looked like a Greek god. All he needed was a toga. "I can't say I recall this occurring on earth, but it has occurred several times in the divine realms."

My head snapped back with surprise. "It has?"

"Oh yes. During several ancient wars, demons have possessed other creatures in attempts to worm their way back into the gates of heaven. During those possessions, the unfortunate victims all had red eyes."

"Daniel! Why didn't you tell us that?"

His eyebrows rose in surprise. "Because you never asked."

I swallowed a groan in frustration and knew I couldn't hold Daniel's peculiar behavior against him.

"So demons, huh?" I shuddered. "That sounds intense."

Daniel arched a perfect eyebrow. "That is one word to describe it."

I put my hands on my hips, eyeing Logan. My boyfriend also wore a disturbed expression.

"Is it possible something like that is happening here on earth?" I asked Daniel. "Could demons be possessing supernaturals?"

Daniel frowned. "I suppose it is possible, but it is not likely. Full-blooded demons are unable to travel to earth. They can only travel through the realms."

"Yet half-blooded demons can travel here," I replied, thinking of Xanthia.

Daniel nodded. "Yes, that is true. Many half demons reside on earth."

Logan's disturbed expression didn't abate. "Could half demons be behind this?"

Daniel shook his head. "No, most definitely not. Possession requires the strength of a full-blooded demon, much like instant teleporting can only be done by full-blooded angels."

"So even though demons haven't traveled to earth before, you still think it's possible that full-blooded demons have found a way to possess supernaturals here on earth?" I asked.

Daniel shrugged. "Anything is possible."

I frowned. "That *would* explain the attack I suffered from the rogues. According to Xanthia, demons like to congregate together, so if Jayden, Niles, and Zach were possessed, that would explain why they were working together and why they had red eyes."

"You're right," Logan said, nodding his head. "That would explain all of that."

"Should we tell Wes?" I asked Logan.

But Logan was already pulling out his tablet. "I'll send him a quick message. He can contact the half demon SF members to see what they know. Even though most half demons avoid full blooded demons in hell, it's possible that some may know how to get in touch with one. Perhaps we can find some answers that way." A pensive look grew on Logan's face.

I cocked my head. "What?"

"If it's true that demons possessed those rogues that attacked you, then that could also explain the strange smell I detected on them." He turned to Daniel. "What do demons smell like?"

Daniel's nose wrinkled. "Like sulfur and rot."

Logan's expression turned grimmer. "That's how they smelled."

After sending a message to Wes, Logan shoved his

tablet back into his pocket. Given the tense way he stood, I knew the red-eyed attacks weighed heavily on his mind.

I eyed my pants again, knowing I needed to change, but I still wanted desperately to erase the worry from my boyfriend's face. "It's about lunchtime, isn't it?"

Daniel cocked his head. "I believe lunch is the meal most humans consume during the middle of the day, is it not? In that case, yes, it is lunchtime."

I stepped closer to Logan. "Have you eaten?"

A frown still marred his striking features, but he shook himself. "No. Have you?"

"Nope. How about I clean up then we head down to the marketplace for a bite to eat? I also wanted to try to find that psychic if we have time. Every time Xanthia and I have been to the marketplace lately, she's been gone." It warmed me to think of Xanthia. Over the past few weeks, we'd started becoming friends.

Logan glanced at his watch, some of the tension easing from his shoulders. "I don't have to report back for another few hours. That would work."

"Great! Give me ten minutes, and I'll be ready to go."

∞ ∞ ∞

Logan and I ventured alone to the supernatural marketplace for lunch. Daniel insisted on staying behind, apparently finding his accommodation on the *bus* quite to his liking.

"What kind of food do you want?" Logan asked when we approached the alleyway leading to the supernatural marketplace portal. We'd parked the SF vehicle we'd borrowed a few blocks away, passing the Mexican café we'd had lunch in with Cecile and Mike the other week.

"What kind of food can we only get in the marketplace? I'm game to try something new."

Logan cocked an eyebrow, his dark eyes twinkling. "Have you ever had dragon stew?"

I stumbled to a stop. "You mean, it has actual *dragon* meat in it?"

He laughed and nodded at the alleyway between the bakery and mom-and-pop hardware store. I resumed walking at his side, albeit not as excitedly.

"No. No dragon meat, I swear. It's just what it's called. Dragon stew is a special concoction that half demons specialize in making. It's quite tasty."

"So if it doesn't have dragon meat, what does it have?"

He shrugged. "I'm not entirely sure, but I do know they use spices that aren't available on earth. I believe they buy them from the fairies."

"So no dragon meat but spices from the fae lands. Okay, I'll try it."

We stepped up to the glowing portal door at the marketplace entrance. To humans, it was invisible, but to supernaturals, the door glimmered as the magical barrier glowed in a red ribbon around it.

"Ready to step through?" Logan hesitated at the threshold.

"I'm ready. Part of my training with Daniel has included portal transfer. With him, it's not nearly as jarring."

As soon as we stepped through the glowing door, I plummeted through space, squeezing, twisting, and popping all at once, but I concentrated on what Daniel had told me—to use my angel powers to diminish the sensations.

I tried to do as he said and let them burst free, but just as quickly as the portal sensations started, they stopped. Logan and I emerged in the marketplace.

My powers rolled in my belly, and with a start, I realized both of them fluttered freely, my light no longer contained in the safety chest deep below my navel.

For a moment, panic consumed me. The dark power responded, rushing up, but then I remembered what Daniel had told me. *Let them become one with you.*

I closed my eyes and took a deep breath, trying to calm the rising panic. I let the dark power rise, leaving it unchecked. I held my breath, not sure what it would do, but it was as if my power knew I wasn't trying to control it.

Similar to my light, it stopped when it reached my palms, not trying to escape my body.

"Whoa," Logan murmured.

I opened my eyes. He smiled down at me with a look of admiration.

With a gasp, I saw that my skin glowed once again, like a glimmering translucent cloud.

"You're beautiful," Logan whispered.

My heart rate increased as power rushed through my veins. The strength of my angel lineage flowed so potently. I felt strong enough to move a mountain, experienced enough to bring a client back from the brink of death, and powerful enough to face a full-blooded demon.

I took shallow breaths as I acclimated to the feeling of my powers being free. The sensation wasn't new to me. Several times during the past week, when I'd been training with Daniel, I'd reached that state, but I'd always been with the angel.

Now, my potential mate stood at my side.

Tentatively, I reached for Logan's hand. I threaded my fingers through his, his body relaxing as his fingers curled around mine.

I closed my eyes, reveling in the feel of him and of my powers. His palm felt warm, deliciously so. Desire surged within my core.

Logan's fingers tightened their grip, another sharp intake of breath from him reaching my ears.

He inhaled deeply. "Roses in heat again."

Hearing the huskiness of his tone made my desire flame hotter. As if knowing that Logan was a potential mate, my light responded, growing dimmer and less strong, relaxing in Logan's presence.

But my dark power was another story. It stayed strong, flowing in cold rivers through my veins, in complete contradiction to the heat of my light.

I opened my eyes and hastily pulled my hand away, not trusting my dark power not to rush forth like it had in my training sessions.

The glowing hue around me disappeared as my old

habits reared their ugly heads. Before I knew what I was doing, I'd pushed my powers back down.

"Ugh!" I groaned in frustration.

"You're getting better. You really are." Logan brushed a finger across my cheek, the movement so brief that it didn't stir my powers again.

I smiled, or tried to. "It's still frustrating, though. Just when I think I'm controlling them, or rather *not* controlling them, something happens, and I panic. The next thing I know, I'm shoving them down again and locking my light away."

"It's hard to undo years of habit."

"I know, but I still wish I could get better at this faster."

He chuckled. "Does this have anything to do with me wanting to touch you?"

"It has *everything* to do with that, and me wanting to touch you too. That, and since I can now kill people, I kinda need *not* to do that."

Logan laughed, a deep sound that had me smiling as tingles raced to my toes.

I placed my hands on my hips. Ahead of us, the marketplace loomed, the familiar cobblestone walkways and narrow streets stretching in front of us. "Should we find that dragon stew?"

Chapter 10

Dragon stew was so good that I actually picked my bowl up and licked it clean. The rich, fragrant soup tasted similar to hearty beef stew, but the smoother texture and creamier consistency made it unique. It also carried a sharp spice that rolled over my tongue, coating my taste buds, like nothing I'd had before.

Logan chuckled when I sighed in bliss, an amused smirk lifting his lips. "I told you it was good."

"You weren't kidding." I snatched the remaining bite of bread from my plate and soaked up the last drop. "It's sooo delicious!" I mumbled around my mouthful of the thick baguette. I finally finished and set my bowl down before wiping my mouth. "What *is* that spice they use?"

Logan shrugged and finished his last spoonful. He'd

ordered three bowls of soup for himself, as usual, his high werewolf metabolism demanding extra calories. "You'd have to ask the fairies."

Around us, other patrons occupied the small cluster of tables at the café. A line also waited at the door. Apparently, we weren't the only ones clamoring for dragon stew.

Behind the counter and in the kitchen, a handful of half demons ran about, serving hungry customers, taking orders, and cooking their various dishes. Similar to Xanthia, they all looked human.

Seeing them reminded me of my half demon friend. Since Xanthia and I had hung out a few times over the past few weeks, she was actually starting to feel like a friend. My first *real* friend I'd ever had. Every time I thought of her bold words and crass remarks, I smiled. She definitely had a memorable personality.

"I'm gonna run to the bathroom. I'll be right back." I rose from my chair, intent on a quick stop at the restroom before we went in search of the psychic. My palms itched at the thought of seeing her again.

As I made my way through the crowded café, a few curious glances and whispered comments followed me.

Like the other times I'd visited the marketplace, my face drew attention. Being the only supernatural healer in the world, I'd come to learn that I was well-known, even if I hadn't known of the community before Logan.

"Excuse me," I mumbled when I bumped into a tall man blocking the path to the bathrooms.

I was about to step past him, but the long coat

covering most of his body made me stop short when I recognized it.

He'd been the man hiding in the trees watching me train. I lifted my head only to find him staring down at me.

"You were watching me earlier." The blunt statement left my mouth before I could stop it.

A wry smile lifted his lips. Because of his sunglasses, I couldn't see his eyes, but his hair was a dull blond, his teeth even, and five o'clock shadow covered his jaw. Up close, he definitely looked middle-aged.

"Daria Gresham," he replied in a quiet voice.

A shiver ran through me. "Do I know you?"

"No, but I know you."

My dark power stirred, obviously sensing my sudden trepidation. "Why were you watching me earlier?"

He leaned against the wall despite the line ahead of him moving closer to the counter. The supernatural behind him grumbled. The mysterious man waved him ahead, but his attention stayed on me.

"I've heard of your angel powers. I wanted to see firsthand how strong they were."

An uneasy flutter tightened my stomach. "Well, as you could see, they're not that great."

"On the contrary, I believe they're something to be reckoned with."

My lips parted, and I was about to ask another question when he pushed away from the wall. "I'm sure we'll meet again." And with that, he strode out of the café.

My breaths came fast as I watched him disappear from view, but as soon as my brain kicked into action, I hurried after him, wanting to know who he was and why I interested him.

Outside, the busy marketplace was a hum of activity. Someone bumped into me, making my power rise. I pushed back against the wall, flattening myself against the café's exterior as I searched for the creepy dude.

But I didn't see him. He'd disappeared into the sea of people, too many supernaturals mingling about for me to catch a clear glimpse of him.

Shaken, I retreated to the café's bathroom before returning to the table Logan and I shared.

"I just had the oddest encounter."

Logan cocked his head after our waitress whisked our dishes away. "What happened?"

I recounted the strange guy I'd just spoken with and how he'd been watching me train. "He said he wanted to see how strong I was getting."

The frown on Logan's face grew. "Do you know who he was?"

I shook my head.

"You didn't catch a name or hear anyone call him anything?"

"No, he was alone both times."

"Describe him to me."

I told him as much as I could recall. "But he wore sunglasses that hid a lot of his face."

Logan leaned back in his chair. "I'll talk to Wes about it when we get back. It may be nothing. He may just be some guy who wanted to see the famous Daria Gresham, but it may be wise to put protection on you while you're training, or even have you train within headquarters."

I tried to imagine training inside the SF, where everyone could watch me spectacularly fail every day. Grimacing, I pushed my hair behind my ears. "Sounds fun." Shaking off that mortifying feeling, I stood again. "Should we try to find the psychic?"

The supernaturals in the café all watched as Logan and I strode toward the door. A few of their gazes raked me up and down.

"Isn't she that Gresham witch?" one woman whispered to her friend when I passed.

I stiffened and kept moving, but I still heard their hushed words as they dipped their heads toward one another.

"I heard she was back. Something about how she thought she was the only supernatural in the world."

Her friend laughed. "What makes her think she's so special?"

Logan stepped closer to my side, blocking me from their view before ushering me out onto the street.

Once we were away from the crowded café, I breathed a little easier, but the women's mocking words still rang in my ears.

Logan's jaw tightened. "Ignore them. They're not worth your time."

"I know, but . . ." I shrugged. "No. You're right." I straightened my shoulders, determined not to let their comments bother me.

The busyness of the marketplace helped distract me. Plenty of people milled about as they did their daily shopping. I kept my eye out for the strange guy.

I figured he'd followed me to the marketplace and for the first time thought Logan's idea to have me train within the SF was probably a smart option, embarrassing or not.

I skipped around a few supernaturals on our way to the psychic's tent, but despite searching down every lane we passed, I never saw the creepy dude again.

When we rounded the corner, I spied the familiar Oriental rugs lining the back wall.

I jogged to it, but my hopes were dashed when I didn't see her. As before, someone else manned it. A teenage boy sat on the stool by the cash register. He held a smartphone and appeared to be playing a game.

"Excuse me?" I stepped directly in front of him.

He brushed his shaggy black hair out of his eyes and regarded me steadily, the game he'd been playing still making noise. "Yeah?"

"Is there a woman with long black hair, blue eyes, and bells around her ankles working here today? I've been trying to find her, but every time I stop by, she's not here."

His expression turned guarded. "Who's asking?"

"I am."

His gaze drifted behind me, to where Logan loomed like a mountain. He looked Logan up and down, his expression turning more wary.

I stepped closer to the boy. "Please. I just want to

speak to her. She's helped me before."

His grip around his phone lessened, his wide eyes becoming hooded again, then he called over his shoulder—"Mom! Someone's here to see you!"—before returning to his video game.

One of the Oriental rugs brushed forward, and the psychic emerged from behind it.

A knowing smile lifted her lips. "Daria Gresham. I see you've returned, and I hear you've been looking for me."

I grinned. *She's finally here!* "Yes, and I followed your advice. I went to that vendor and entered the portal. I met Daniel. In fact, he's with me now."

"He is?" She looked around my shoulder and up and down the marketplace streets. The excitement on her face dimmed when she didn't see him. "Where?"

"Well, not with me at this exact moment, but he's staying with me."

"Oh. I see. Perhaps you could bring him by one day. I would like to meet him."

I shifted my weight from one foot to the other. "Sure. I'll try to do that, but right now, I really need you to answer some questions for me."

Her expression turned passive again. "Do you always travel with SF members?"

"You know that Logan's part of the SF?" Every time I spoke with the woman, she surprised me more and more. The fact that she knew about angels, the portal Victor guarded, and Emunda was vastly more than any supernatural I'd met, *and* she also knew Logan's occupation.

"I know many things."

Clearly. "That's exactly why I'm here. I'm hoping you can answer some questions for me."

She pushed her long dark hair over her shoulders, her bright-blue eyes assessing me shrewdly. "Information doesn't come freely, as I warned you last time. The other times I spoke with you were out of the goodness of my heart, but I must charge for my services."

I stuffed my hands into my pockets, fumbling for money. "Of course. I'll pay you. How much do you charge?"

She crossed her arms, her long nails like claws. "What is it you wish to know?"

"What happened to my family hundreds of years ago, after they left the community and disappeared from Europe?"

Her eyes brightened with interest. "That's a very intriguing question."

I waited for her to continue, but she kept staring at me, her sapphire gaze unwavering.

"Do you know the answer to that?" I asked.

"I may."

I avoided the urge to roll my eyes. "How much?"

"Two hundred."

I balked. Even when my healing tours went well and my clients were able to pay more than we'd hoped, I still didn't have that kind of cash on hand. And since I wasn't working, I *really* didn't have that much.

My shoulders slumped. "I don't have that kind of

money right now."

"Let me." Logan pulled his wallet out.

I should have shaken my head and told him that he didn't have to pay, but desperation to know more about my family made all of my pride fly out the window.

As if knowing my thoughts, the psychic said, "You should let him pay for you and not feel bad about it. You've ensnared his heart. Women have great power over men when that happens."

For a moment, I was speechless, then I managed to mumble, "That doesn't mean I should take advantage of him."

She cocked her head. "Doesn't it?"

Logan tensed, probably since we were talking about him like he wasn't there, before he shoved the money into the psychic's hand. "Two hundred. It's all there if you want to count it."

She slipped the money into a fold of her skirt. "I trust you. You're an SF member after all. Now, my dear, what do you wish to know?"

I repeated the question I'd asked earlier. "What happened to my family hundreds of years ago, after they left the community and disappeared from Europe?"

"They came here."

"To the community?"

"No, to America. It was the New World back then, a world full of possibilities, but also the perfect place to hide. Here, they were nobody. Nobody knew their history or what they were. The Gresham women were safe here as long as they remained in hiding."

My heart pounded harder. I licked my lips, which had suddenly gone dry. "And what about the dark power? How did they get rid of it?"

She glanced down, looking at my hands. "You aren't wearing your family's ring."

"My family's ring? But how do you know about that?" I'd never seen the heirloom that had been passed down from generation to generation—a large emerald ring set in a simple setting with a swirly Celtic pattern on the band. I'd thought I would see it when Dillon Parker had lured me to his mobile home, but that had been a lie. "No. It was lost long ago."

"That's a shame."

"Why? What does the ring do?"

The psychic fingered the fold in her skirt. "If you'd like more information, I'll need another two hundred."

My jaw dropped just as Logan said, "She already paid you that. I think you can tell her more than what you have."

The psychic laughed. "The SF member is trying to haggle. Oh, how divine. But no, Major Smith. That's not how it works. I set the price. For more information, I need another two hundred dollars. If not, my lips are sealed."

I seethed inwardly, but I also knew she had all the power. "I'll be back. With enough money so you can tell me *everything* I want to know."

She dipped her head. "As you wish."

The familiar phrase made me pause. I had no idea if she was saying it in a mocking tone, since she apparently knew of angels, or if she truly meant it.

"Will you still be here in twenty minutes?" I asked.

"Possibly. Sometimes I need to leave unexpectedly. It's hard to say."

Her cryptic answers only made the nerves in my stomach flutter more. She knew about my family's ring, and she'd asked about it when I wanted to know about the dark power.

That had to mean something.

I was about to turn away when she abruptly grabbed my arm. My powers tingled, both battering my insides. She removed her hand, as if sensing them. "There is something, though, that I need to tell you now."

Her alert yet mysterious expression morphed into a vacant daze. She stared off in the distance, her arms dangling listlessly at her sides. When she opened her mouth to speak, her voice changed, becoming deeper and more monotone.

"A war is coming. A war between the dark and the light. Take care, my young angel. Dangerous times are ahead."

My lips parted, and for a moment, I couldn't breathe.

The psychic blinked then shook herself, as if coming out of a trance. She smoothed back her hair, but her hand shook. "You come back when you have that money." Before I could ask her about what she'd just predicted, she turned and disappeared behind one of the Oriental rugs.

I lunged forward. "Wait!"

Her son moved in front of me before I could pull the

rug back. "You're not allowed back there."

From his body's stance and the firm tightness of his jaw, I knew he wouldn't budge. "What did she mean by that?" I asked.

He shrugged. "No idea. You'd better come back with more money if you want to find out." He returned to his stool, the game on his smartphone again holding his attention.

Wrapping my arms around myself, I turned back to Logan, who looked troubled.

We left the shop in a hurry. I could only hope the psychic would still be there after we found more cash.

But I was in such a daze, that I didn't realize someone blocked my path until I almost walked right into her.

"I can't believe they let you out." The woman sneered.

I sucked in a breath when I came eye to eye with Chloe. The fairy stood with her arms crossed, her spiky red hair jutting up at odd angles. I hadn't seen her since that awful day I'd blasted Phoenix and she'd come to the recovery room with the rest of her squad.

"What are you doing here?" Logan growled.

Chloe flashed her sharp teeth at him. "None of your business, wolf. It's a public place, isn't it?"

He stepped forward. "Not now, Chloe. It hasn't been a good morning for Daria."

Her eyebrows shot up before drawing together in a scowl. "Are you fucking kidding me? You're walking next to a ticking time bomb, and all you care about is if she's had a good day?"

I shrank back, taking a step away from Chloe. Between the hostility floating off her and the psychic's disturbing words, I shook like a leaf.

Logan's voice lowered. "Not now, Chloe."

Her cool blue eyes narrowed. "I mean it, Logan. She shouldn't be out here."

"She's much better. You don't know what the hell you're talking about."

Hearing him defend me, and his absolute conviction that I wouldn't hurt anybody, had me standing straighter. "He's right, Chloe. I'm getting better, and I really am sorry for what I did to Phoenix the other week. I didn't mean to. Honestly, it was an accident."

Hostility still rose off Chloe in waves. "I'll believe it when I see it. Until then, I don't think you're safe to be in public. I'm surprised Wes even lets you leave headquarters."

"She's not a prisoner." Logan stepped in front of me, cutting off my view. In a way, it reminded me of when he'd been my bodyguard.

Chloe smirked. "Whatever, Logan. You can call it whatever you want, but we all know that if you weren't getting in her pants, you'd feel the same as the rest of us. She's not safe. She should be locked up until she learns how to control herself."

Before Logan or I could respond, Chloe turned and stormed off.

Even though I knew I was getting better, and that sooner or later I would learn to live with my powers as well as Daniel, her comments still cut to the quick. I wrapped my arms around myself.

"Don't listen to her," Logan said quietly.

I took a deep breath. "I know I'm not as dangerous as she's claiming, but she's partly right." I shook my head. "Is it crazy that I thought I would fit in here in the community? I've never fit in anywhere, but I thought maybe, just maybe, I'd finally fit in here among other supernaturals." I forced a shaky smile. "But even here, I'm too different."

His gaze softened, and he brushed a finger across my cheek. My powers didn't respond.

"Don't let her get in your head. That's not true. You *do* fit in here, and you're doing fantastic. You've only been training for two weeks, and look at the progress you've already made. Imagine what you'll be like in another month."

Hearing his complete conviction and absolute faith in me helped dislodge the lump in my throat. Taking a deep breath, I nodded. "You're right. I just need to keep reminding myself that."

"Now, let's get that money—" Logan's cell phone rang. With a frown, he pulled it out of his pocket and brought it to his ear. "Smith."

Rapid words came from the caller, but I couldn't make them out.

A heavy scowl grew on Logan's face. "I'll be right there." He shoved his phone back into his pocket, and my stomach sank.

"What's wrong?" I asked, thinking of the psychic's chilling premonition.

Logan took a deep breath, worry in his eyes. "We have to go back to headquarters. There's been another attack."

Chapter 11

"There's been another attack? Already?" I panted as we hurried to the portal. "But there was one last night. They've never happened back to back before."

Logan jogged at my side. "And this latest attack wasn't far from here. That's a first. All the others occurred far away. It seems whoever we're up against is growing bolder. Everybody knows that our headquarters are in Boise, and most criminals steer clear of this entire state."

"How close was it?"

"Around fifty miles north."

"Did anyone die?"

His jaw tightened. "Two. A werewolf and a sorcerer. Both SF members. Wes said they were burned to death and that the burn marks were unusual."

"How were they unusual?"

"They were completely cremated. That kind of burn is typically only inflicted by one creature—dragons."

"What? A dragon is *here* on earth? That's not normal, right?"

"No. That's never happened."

I pushed my hair out of my eyes as we reached the portal door, knowing any hope of getting more information from the psychic that afternoon was gone.

Between the glowing red eyes, which according to Daniel potentially meant demon possession, and the use of a dragon in the latest attack, one thing was becoming apparent—the attacks involved divine creatures.

And since I'm a divine creature . . .

I faltered mid-step.

According to Daniel, my dark power was created to banish evil. Demons were pure evil, and I'd definitely had no trouble with Jayden and Niles when they attacked. If they *had* been possessed by demons . . .

That explains my powers' reaction to them.

I bit my lip. I had the power to banish demons if needed, which meant I could potentially be an asset to whatever was going on.

The psychic's words came back to haunt me. *A war is coming. A war between the dark and the light. Take care, my young angel. Dangerous times are ahead.*

I closed my eyes as the portal sucked us in, my thoughts spinning faster than the portal winds.

∞ ∞ ∞

When we reached headquarters, Brodie, Alexander, Jake, and Xanthia were all waiting. Xanthia's hands were balled into fists, and she fumed from where she stood.

"They're using *my* dragon—that they *stole*—to kill innocent people!" She paced the processing room, her heavy boots clomping on the floor as she rolled her tongue piercing over and over between her teeth.

"But how did the dragon get to earth?" Alexander stood with his arms crossed. "That's the more important question. Dragons have never left the underworld before."

My eyebrows shot up as I held my wrist out for Millie. Lasers erupted from her device that verified my identity.

"So it's truly confirmed then. Your dragon is definitely here?" I asked.

Xanthia sighed heavily and stopped pacing. "She has to be. Those burn marks were dragon burns." She resumed her pacing, her black cargo pants swishing against her legs. "Whoever stole Quaneely must have had help. I've never heard of dragons leaving the divine realms."

"Then there's the red-eyed supes that, rumor has it, are possessed by demons," Jake added. "And last I heard, demons weren't supposed to be able to leave the realms, either, so how the hell are they here on earth?"

"No pun intended," Brodie said with a sly grin.

Wes appeared in the doorway and walked briskly

toward us. The tablet he carried glowed, the screen revealing a long report.

"Regardless of dragons and demons never threatening earth before," the SF general said, "that's not the case now. I've just confirmed that it was indeed demons possessing the red-eyed supernaturals. Master Gregor found several old texts about an incident that occurred over two thousand years ago. It was buried so deeply in the history books that I'm not surprised no one's heard of this happening. During that incident, demons had possessed fairies in the fae lands, just as Daniel said. Only now, it's happening on earth."

Millie finished checking in Logan and stepped back, her usual cheerful smile absent. She shakily set her tablet on the perimeter bench.

Logan put his watch back on, having taken it off for the scan. "Are there any clues as to who's behind this?"

"Not yet," Wes replied.

I placed my hands on my hips. "I should tell Daniel. He may be able to help."

Brodie nodded. "Good call, Dar. Lover Boy probably knows all about his hot-blooded friends from the underworld."

"Wes? Are you okay with that?" I asked Logan's boss.

Wes pursed his lips. "I can give both of you clearance for the next week. Since you and Daniel can kill demons with your angelic powers, and considering Daniel is the one who informed us about the demon possession, I think having you both involved is reasonable. Although per protocol, you'll both have to pass background and security checks."

I cleared my throat awkwardly. "Are you saying we'll be SF *staff?*"

"More or less. Although the technical term is *consultants*. You won't be actual SF members, rather outside staff we consult with."

"And regarding the security checks, is that possible for a full-blooded angel who's never been to earth before?" I asked.

"Even if we can't find any information on Daniel, protocol is protocol," Wes replied. "We'll still try."

"Okay, then let me find him and see if he's willing to help." I paused, remembering how Daniel said that if I ever needed him, all I needed to do was call.

I stepped away from the group, intending to walk into the outer hall so I could have some privacy. After all, I had no idea how loudly I needed to call for my angel trainer.

I ducked around the corner so nobody would see me yelling if it came to that. Once I stood at least fifty feet away, I raised my voice. "Daniel? I need you."

I waited.

Nothing happened.

After clearing my throat, I said louder, "Daniel, I—"

"No need to yell, young angel. I'm right here."

I twirled around, my long blond hair brushing against my upper arms. Daniel leaned against the hallway's concrete wall, the harsh fluorescent lights making his skin glow golden. For anybody else, the lighting would have highlighted every flaw, every clogged pore, and every imperfection, but as usual, Daniel looked nothing but perfect.

"Thanks for coming." I crossed my arms. "I need your help."

"Of course. How may I assist you?"

"There's been another attack by red-eyed supes. Wes confirmed that demon possessions are definitely occurring, and now a dragon is on earth too. Do you think you can help us? Wes said he'd welcome any help you can give."

He dipped his head. "As you wish."

I led Daniel around the corner and back to the group. Everyone still stood in the processing room. When we emerged, Logan's sandalwood scent caught my attention. He paced near the far wall, a heavy frown on his face. A vent hummed above him, cool air filtering through, wafting his scent in my direction.

"Daria!" Xanthia strode purposefully toward me as the rest of Logan's squad members and Wes stood in a circle, discussing something. She gave Daniel the once-over when she reached us, her bright-blue eyes appraising him. "Good, you're here, and wow, that was quick. How did you get here so fast?"

"I teleported."

Xanthia rolled her tongue piercing between her teeth again. "Oh, right. Sweet. A few demons can do that, too, but not outside of the divine realms. But angels can do it even on earth, eh? Handy."

She returned her attention to me just as Logan approached us. "We've been talking," Xanthia said, "and since you're part angel, I think what we have in mind will work."

I studied her, not understanding what she meant. Logan placed his hands on his hips, giving Xanthia a firm shake of his head.

"Relax," Xanthia chided Logan. "Daria's a big girl. She'll be fine."

"Fine for what?" I asked. "And why does it matter that I'm part angel?"

"Because Wes and I both think that if it isn't a demon behind the attacks, then whoever *is* behind it has to have a demon on his payroll. Only an uber-important demon would be able to find a way to transport dragons to earth, and most demons, at least the big, important ones, never leave hell."

"Okay . . ." I said hesitantly. From the dark expression forming on Logan's face, I already knew he wasn't a fan of whatever plan Xanthia and Wes had come up with.

"So I'm going back to hell," Xanthia continued. "I need to check on my other dragons, and I'm also going to see what I can find about the demon behind all this. Which means that I could use some extra help. You know, three minds are better than one, so I want you and Daniel to come with me."

"Not happening." Logan's loud statement made me jump.

Xanthia rolled her eyes. "But she's a divine creature. She can travel between the realms, and Daniel's powers could be invaluable if we get into trouble."

Logan gritted his teeth. "Like I said earlier to you and Wes, it's not happening. Daria's not a trained fighter. She's a healer. Her place is *here*, on earth, even if she's part angel."

My heart thumped wildly at the thought of leaving earth to visit dragons and chase demons. But Xanthia was right. I was an angel. I was made to fight exactly what we were up against.

Still, how crazy everything in my life had become.

Only two months ago, I lived on a tour bus and drove around the country, healing people, and the most exciting thing I did on Friday nights was watch old reruns with Cecile or Mike.

Now, I was contemplating traveling to the underworld with a half demon and a full-blooded angel to check on dragons and try to find the high-powered demon behind the attacks.

I shook my head, forcing myself back to the present.

"I don't know," I finally replied. "Logan's right. I'm not trained. I can barely control my powers as it is. I'm not sure how much help I would be."

Something flashed in the depths of her blazing sapphire eyes, something she was trying desperately to hide before she replied with false bravado, "All right. Sure, no worries. I can go alone."

But she hadn't veiled that look fast enough—I saw her fear.

Xanthia was *afraid* to go alone.

That realization made my heart thump faster. If there was one thing I'd learned about my new friend in the previous two weeks, it was that not much fazed her.

My dark power rolled inside me, rattling in my belly and wanting out. I could feel its strength and its power. My dark power was ready to fight evil after centuries of being locked away.

I reminded myself that it had rushed to my aid when I'd been threatened by not one, but *three* demon-possessed supernaturals, and that was before I knew anything about it or had any idea how to wield it.

And after only two weeks of intense training with Daniel, while I certainly wasn't a master at it, I had learned a thing or two.

I couldn't ignore the fact that I had one of the strongest and most natural gifts in the world, and that it was created to banish exactly what we were after.

Eyeing Logan again, I took a deep breath. "You know what, on second thought, I think Xanthia's right. She shouldn't do this alone. I'm going with her."

"What?" Logan's eyes blazed. "No."

I stepped closer to him, raising a palm to his chest. I felt mostly certain that I could touch him for brief periods of time without blasting him to bits. I settled my hand on his chest, feeling his muscles jump. "I'll be fine. Daniel will be with me, and Xanthia knows what she's doing in the underworld."

"But Dar . . ." Logan's pleading tone was nearly my undoing. Stark fear etched into his features.

"Trust me, Logan. Please. I'm not as helpless or as weak as you think I am."

"I don't think you're weak or helpless."

"Perhaps, but it kinda comes off that way. And I know you're afraid for me, but that fear stems more from *you*. I'm actually pretty capable. Don't forget, I killed two demon-possessed supernaturals with my bare hands, and that was before I even knew what I was doing. Not that I actually know what I'm doing now." I muttered that last bit under my breath.

"I'll watch out for her." Daniel stepped closer to my side.

I flashed him a grateful look.

But Logan's jaw still tightened, the muscle ticking in its corner. "I'm not going to change your mind, am I?"

"No."

He pulled me tightly into his arms, his heat surrounding me, his scent everywhere. "In that case, be careful, and always know where your exit portals are. If shit hits the fan, don't be the hero. Run. Get back to that portal as fast as you can."

I closed my eyes, relishing the feel of his hard chest pressed against mine and the strength of his grip. Amazingly, my powers stayed calm. *See, I'm getting better at this.*

"I'll be careful. You stay safe too."

When he pulled back, he seemed reluctant to let me go, but Xanthia's tapping foot and constant glances at her watch reminded us that the world kept turning.

"Do you know where you're going?" Logan asked her.

She rolled her eyes. "Dude, I've spent years of my life in hell. *Of course* I know where I'm going."

Logan nodded curtly and gave me one last desperate look.

I squeezed his hand. "See you soon."

Chapter 12

After Wes secured Daniel and me as official short-term SF consultants, we left headquarters and traveled to the heart of Boise in an SF sedan.

Xanthia pulled the sedan into a McDonald's parking lot and cut the engine.

"Are we getting Big Macs before we go?" I glanced at the drive-through.

Xanthia laughed, her eyes twinkling. "I hadn't intended to, but now that you mention it, french fries do sound good." She pointed at a darkened corner of the parking lot. "See that over there? That's the nearest portal door to hell."

My eyebrows shot up. "Seriously? There's a portal door right here in the middle of town?"

"Yep. Seriously. The portals are in the most surprising places. There's one in California at a public botanical gardens. The groundskeepers are always replanting around it. I'm sure it's baffling to them why the plants by it keep dying."

"It's been a while since I have ventured to the underworld." Daniel sat stiffly in his seat, a faint glow emitting from his skin. "I can only hope our maker will approve of this little venture. Usually, we are not allowed to visit the underworld unless we are instructed to."

I leaned forward from where I sat in the backseat and put my hand on Daniel's shoulder. "Are you sure you can go? Is this going to cause problems for you? I know the only reason you're helping me is to try to get in our maker's good graces again so you can resume living in heaven."

Daniel gave my hand a placating pat. "Don't fear, my young angel. All will be well."

"Are you two ready?" Xanthia took off her seatbelt and opened her door. "It's kinda hot down there, Daria. I hope you're ready to sweat." She gave me a wicked grin.

I stopped unbuckling my seatbelt. "Wait a minute—will I be able to tolerate the heat?"

Xanthia laughed. "Of course you will. I'm just messing with you."

The three of us stepped out of the vehicle, and the cool nighttime air swirled around us. A line of cars waited at the drive-through. Most likely, the occupants were all normal humans out for a late-night snack.

I stepped closer to Xanthia and asked quietly, "What

if they see us disappear into the portal?"

She just shook her head and continued walking across the parking lot, her loud boots stomping on the pavement. "They won't see anything unusual. I keep forgetting that you're new to the community and don't understand how everything works. Did Logan ever explain to you about sorcerer magic and how it interferes with human memories?"

I nodded. "Yeah, he told me all about that. Does that mean that all portal doors have been secured with sorcerer magic?"

Xanthia smiled. "Bingo. If any of those people happen to glance over here while we disappear into the portal, all they'll see are three people walking toward the parking lot corner then continuing on down the alleyway back there. They won't see us disappear."

When we reached the portal, I could make out its faint lines. They glowed dark, like a glittery silver line, barely visible in the night.

I shivered. "Are all portal doors different colors?"

"Yep, the color deems the classification," Xanthia replied. "Red portal doors were created by supernatural creatures here on earth, silvery black ones go to hell, and green is to the fae lands."

"And purple goes to Emunda?" I asked.

Xanthia's eyebrows knit together. "Emunda?"

"The land of lost angels," Daniel informed her. "And that's correct, Daria. Emunda portals are violet."

Daniel's skin glowed brighter, and my dark power rattled wildly. I clamped a hand over my belly, my eyes widening. "What's happening, Daniel? I'm struggling to keep my dark power from bursting free."

His face glowed as beautifully as a sunset when he turned my way. "We're too close to the underworld to control it now. I can no longer temper my powers, either. Let them free, young angel. Don't fight them. It's imperative that when we step into hell, you don't fight your natural instincts. They are what will keep you alive."

Never having seen Daniel so serious before, I shivered. What we were doing was suddenly becoming real.

I was about to enter hell and come face-to-face with full-blooded demons.

Powerful demons.

Demons who had the power to pass dragons through the portals.

I wasn't so naïve to think they would let us pass by freely. The fact that Xanthia had felt reluctant to do the job on her own when she worked in the underworld spoke volumes of the dangers ahead.

I took one last look over my shoulder at the McDonald's and the surrounding buildings. Since we stood so closely to the portal door, I knew the sorcerer magic was already at work. Nobody could see us, but I could see them.

A teenage boy and girl pushed through the exit door at the fast food joint, laughing and holding hands. They looked so carefree and happy, having no idea that only a dozen yards away lay a door to the devil himself.

A brief pang of remorse hit me. My life in the human

world had truly come to an end. There was no going back after knowing all that I did. Yet I still had clients that counted on me. I still had a waiting list. Somehow, I would have to return to help them.

But that was a problem for another day.

"Are you ready, Daria?" Xanthia's dry humor had evaporated, her eyes taking on a wild look.

I nodded shakily. "As ready as I'll ever be."

Chapter 13

The journey through the portal door was ten times worse than anything I'd experienced before.

When the portal sucked us into its dark embrace, all hell broke loose. A force like a tidal wave slammed down on my body, pushing me deeper and deeper into a void that felt like suffocating quicksand. I tried to keep ahold of Daniel's hand, but my grip became impossible to maintain.

I felt as if I were being squeezed under immense pressure, as though venturing to the deepest depths of the ocean, where the pressure was so great that human life could not survive.

I tried to breathe, tried to scream, tried to call for Xanthia or Daniel, but no words came out.

My dark power unleashed itself, but unlike the other portal transfers, the underworld one did not end quickly. The only thing that kept me from falling into a chasm of terror was feeling the strengths of my dark and light powers inside me. They hummed and swelled, growing more potent as every second ticked by.

Just when I thought my heart would burst from the intense pressure, the portal ended. Out of nowhere, I fell onto all fours, landing on something hot and smoky. I panted heavily, my lungs filling with thick sooty air that tasted as hot as fire. The intensely hot ground rumbled and shook, trembling beneath my palms.

I shot to my feet and glanced around, my eyes widening. "Daniel! Xanthia!"

My chest rose faster and faster with each gulp of scorching air. The sky was darker than night and devoid of any stars or moons. Black, volcanic-looking rock covered the ground, butting up to distant mountains shooting fire and ash on the horizon. And the ground was as rocky and hot as a volcano, fury fires spouting from small crevices, casting the entire area into fields of erupting molten lava.

And the *heat*—it was so intense, it felt as if my clothes would catch on fire.

Surprisingly, I wasn't sweating, but my skin *felt* like it could melt, and I had a feeling, if I were fully human, it would have.

I whirled around again, searching for my friends. My heart jumped into my throat when I still didn't see them.

I took a tentative step away from the portal door,

terrified I would lose sight of it and would be trapped in the underworld forever.

"Daniel! Xanthia!" I called again.

"There you are!"

I spun around to see Xanthia appear from around a large black boulder through a smoky fog, Daniel on her tail.

"Thank the heavens," Daniel said when he reached my side. "You took longer than us to travel through the portal. We have been looking for you since you did not emerge right after us. I feared you had been misplaced and had come through another portal door."

I took a deep, shaky breath, my panic easing. Fire still filled my lungs with each inhalation, but it didn't hurt. "That transfer did seem to take longer than most."

Xanthia nodded vigorously. "For a few minutes there, we thought you weren't going to make it. You know, since you're half angel and all. I kinda wondered if maybe the portal rejected you."

I dusted my knees off. Sooty material clung to my pants. "Why would it have rejected me?"

Xanthia and Daniel shared concerned looks as the ground continued to rumble. I hoped that was normal.

Daniel cleared his throat. "I had assumed you would have no problems venturing to this realm since you ventured to Emunda so easily. However, half-bloods have occasionally not survived portal realm transfers. When that has occurred, they have never emerged."

My eyes bulged. "And you're only telling me this *now?*"

Xanthia gave me a shaky smile. "Sorry. I guess that's something we should have warned you about."

Daniel dipped his head. "I have failed you, my young angel. You have my deepest apologies."

I was about to reply, but something appeared behind him and Xanthia. I took a shaky step back. "Guys?" I pointed over their shoulders. "Is that anything to worry about?"

Xanthia twirled around as a huge creature with leathery black skin, glowing red eyes, a gaping mouth filled with razor-sharp teeth, and six horns protruding from its skull crested a slope and ran straight toward us. Huge claws extended from its fingers on its short arms like some kind of mutated T. rex.

A menacing smile lifted Xanthia's lips. "And the fun begins."

From out of her back pocket, Xanthia withdrew something small and coiled. With a flick of her wrist, a long glowing rope appeared in her hand. "I knew the chikabons wouldn't be welcoming us, but I didn't think they'd find us this quickly."

"The what?" I backed up more.

The ground rumbled again when Xanthia replied, "They're chikabons. Creatures of the underworld that devour souls not meant to be here. I'm sure your blond hair and aqua eyes and, you know, that glowing-skin thing you've got going on right now are probably why. To them, you probably look like raw meat to a starving dog."

The chikabon *did* seem to be focusing on me and Daniel as it closed in. I breathed harder, becoming more aware of my dark and light. My powers flowed strongly through my limbs, and similar to when I'd been in Emunda, my skin glowed brightly. It suddenly struck me that perhaps I didn't need to cower after all.

"So that thing is going to try to eat us?" I asked.

The ground rumbled again, more so with every leaping step the chikabon took.

"Yep," Xanthia replied, a wicked grin growing on her face. "Nothing like being home sweet home." With a flick of her wrist, her glowing lasso grew in length, sparks emitting from the end.

"Shouldn't we run?"

"Run?" Xanthia laughed. "Why would we do that?"

Daniel crouched down, his hands balling into fists as his shoulders shifted. Something beneath his shirt rippled.

I sucked in a yelp as huge wings sprouted from his back, splitting right through his shirt and ripping the fabric in two. The tattered cloth fell to the ground, revealing a perfectly sculpted glowing chest and magnificent beautiful feathery wings spanning at least twelve feet.

His eyebrows drew together darkly, his jaw clenching in a harsh line.

My breath caught. Gone was the gentle, serene angel that I had known previously. In its place, an angel full of vengeance and wrath had been born.

But I didn't have time to stare. Daniel shot into the air, flying at least fifty feet up.

The chikabon picked up its pace, beginning to run in earnest, head down, horns blazing, as its glowing red eyes stared directly at me.

Daniel flapped his wings, staying aloft, his attention focused entirely on the demonic creature, while Xanthia raised her lasso over her head, her wicked grin growing broader.

"Get ready for a little battle, Dar. Damn, it's good to be home."

Chapter 14

I didn't know if I should help or try to stay out of the way. The chikabon was upon us before I knew it, but with a deft flick of her hand, Xanthia's glowing lasso grazed the creature's chest, leaving a deep gash that drew black blood.

The demonic creature dropped its head and roared, an earsplitting, bone-chilling sound that brought chills to my spine despite the heat.

Before the chikabon had a chance to recover from Xanthia's lash, Daniel swooped down from the sky and landed on its shoulders, grasping its horns.

The chikabon flung itself from side to side, trying to dislodge the angel. Its short arms couldn't reach above its head, but it kept trying. Black claws, at least a foot long each, thrashed and clawed at Daniel but couldn't reach him.

Xanthia brought back her lasso and cracked it again. Another deep gash sprouted along the chikabon's thigh, blood pouring down its leg to its hooved foot.

The demonic creature emitted another cry.

I resisted the urge to cover my ears and watched in horror as Daniel leaped from the creature's head to the front of its body.

I shrieked when the chikabon raised its hand to claw him away.

But just as one of the humongous claws reached for Daniel, my angel friend punched his fist into the chikabon's chest and extracted a beating organ.

The demonic creature crumpled to its pointy knees, and Daniel flew away, his magnificent wings flapping.

I panted harshly, my powers flowing so strongly through me that I barely felt in control of myself.

With a thunderous thump, the chikabon landed face-first on the rocky ground before it turned into smoky ash and disappeared in the hot breeze.

"Holy shit," I whispered.

Xanthia coiled her glowing lasso just as Daniel landed a few feet away from me. For someone who had just killed a demonic creature that towered to at least thirty feet, he looked strangely unaffected.

Daniel grasped the beating organ that he had ripped out of the demon's chest in his hand. The pulsing organ was the only thing left of the creature.

With a rush of power, the glow along Daniel's skin

intensified. A loud pop followed, and the organ splattered in Daniel's palm, dark liquid shooting out of it.

After that, like the chikabon, it turned into smoky ash and disappeared.

"What just happened?" I asked.

Xanthia took her neatly coiled lasso, which had shortened to fit perfectly in her palm, and tucked it into her back pocket. "Well, you've just had your first official welcome to the underworld. It just wouldn't be home if something didn't try to kill us the second we arrived."

She looked strangely excited, her blue eyes glittering with glee. I had a feeling I was seeing more of the demonic side of my friend than the psychic side. From what I remembered, of the little I'd read of demons, they thrived on chaos.

Shaking that thought off, I stared at the pulverized demon's organ. "What *was* that?"

"That was his heart," Xanthia replied.

Wiping his hands, Daniel straightened, his huge wings folding behind his back, before he walked to my side. "Are you all right, young angel?"

I nodded shakily. "Yeah, I'm fine, but are you sure I should be here? I was absolutely no help whatsoever with that thing. Maybe I should go back." I eyed the portal door longingly. "I might just hold you guys up and be more of a liability than an asset."

"I go where you go," Daniel replied.

Some of the excitement in Xanthia's eyes dimmed. "You're leaving? Already?"

Seeing that sense of fear creep into her expression

again, I quickly shook my head. "Of course not. I just didn't want to get in the way."

"You're stronger than you think." Daniel stepped closer and lifted my hand in his. Strangely, none of the chikabon's blood covered his skin. His flesh was as clean and glowing as a baby's bottom. "Did you not feel the power flowing inside you when that demon advanced? Look at your skin, young angel. Your powers are right there, waiting for you to tap into them. Trust yourself. Follow your instincts."

I took another deep breath and concentrated on the feel of my powers. They flowed as they had in Emunda. That storage chest that I had created deep in my belly no longer existed. My dark and light powers moved freely, mixing, just below the surface of my skin. A feeling of absolute power rippled through me.

I flipped my hands back and forth. "You're right. I *can* feel it."

Daniel tipped his head in approval. "You're strong, young angel. Much stronger than you think. Trust your instincts. Let them guide you."

Hearing that reminded me of when Jayden, Niles, and Zach had attacked me. In the heat of the moment, a voice had spoken inside my head, telling me what to do.

I still didn't know what caused that voice, but I had listened to it. It had kept me alive.

Daniel was right.

I needed to trust myself and listen to my instincts. Straightening, I resolved not to be so passive the next time something came at us. I wasn't going to let my friends put themselves in harm's way to protect me.

Xanthia cocked her hip, her smile back in place. "Now, are you ready to meet some dragons?"

Chapter 15

Daniel, Xanthia, and I jogged toward the mountains, distant demonic roars and bloodcurdling screams—that sounded eerily human—echoed off the vast canyon walls. Where those screams came from, I had no idea.

As if sensing my unease, Xanthia explained. "Souls of the damned. That's what you're hearing. The gates to hell are right over there." She pointed to the right. "I'd recommend that you avoid that place."

"But isn't that where your dragons are? Don't they guard the gates?"

"Yep, the ones I've trained guard a few of the gates, but the ones I'm currently working with are still too young. They aren't guardians yet."

Daniel ran at my other side, his long arms brushing

the feathered tips of his folded wings. His head continually moved back and forth, his turquoise eyes alert and his mouth tense, as if he was waiting for the next attack.

"How come no more chikabons are coming for us?" I asked, panting.

Xanthia shrugged. "Who knows. Maybe other supes that aren't supposed to be here have entered the portals, so they're currently attacking them. Or maybe a few were watching to see how we handled the first one. They're vicious creatures, but they're not stupid. Daniel handled that one so effectively that I wouldn't be surprised if word has spread that an angel is in our midst. They may be leaving us alone right now, but it won't stay that way. Most likely, they're gathering numbers so their next attack isn't so easy. Whatever the case, we need to hurry. The sooner we get out of here, the better."

I shuddered, imagining a hundred chikabons coming for us. "Right. So what's the plan exactly? I know you want to check on your dragons, but then what?"

She took a deep breath, but her voice remained steady despite the pace. "Then we find any high-ranking demon and hope that he talks to us. All the high-ranking demons are in continual competition with each other. If one of them is involved in what's happening on earth, most likely, the other high-ranking ones know. And if they discover that the angels are after him, it's possible they'll help us so he'll be taken down. That, of course, leaves room for another demon to move even higher up in the ranks. There's no loyalty here. It's every creature for itself."

"How will you know that the demon we talk to isn't the one behind all of this?"

Xanthia tensed, that fear returning to her eyes. "We don't."

"And what happens if he is?"

Her jaw locked. "Then we hope like hell we make it out of here alive."

Suddenly, I understood why she didn't want to venture to the underworld alone. I could only imagine what a high-ranking demon was like if the chikabon—a low-ranking demon, from the sound of it—was what we had encountered upon our arrival.

"How much longer?" Daniel asked.

"It's just over this crest. We're almost there."

Hot smoke rose from a crevasse. I leaped over it. "I hope this doesn't sound offensive, Xanthia, but how do you live here? I mean, how are you able to sleep with all the demons around? Aren't you worried they'll kill you?"

Xanthia laughed and slowed her pace until we were all walking and panting, well, except Daniel, who seemed strangely immune to human exertion. "They don't bother me. The only reason they attacked when we first got here was because of you two. I mean, don't get me wrong—we have our scuffles every now then, which is why I always carry my lasso, but they don't usually try to kill me. At the moment, since I'm traveling with you both, that's another story. But normally, when I'm doing my job here, they leave me alone because I have protection."

"Who protects you?" I asked.

"Lucifer."

I shivered despite the raging heat just as we crested the hill, but what I saw on the other side made my jaw drop. A huge corral covered in a mesh-like dome stretched at least a quarter of a mile. Enclosed within it lay a dozen dragons.

Xanthia sighed. "My babies."

She took off at a run down the hill, then Daniel and I kicked into action. We followed her over the jagged terrain and spewing crevices. Twice, I almost ran right into a geyser of fire but managed to jump out of the way at the last second.

We got to the bottom, and Xanthia approached the domed corral. She kept looking around, her expression growing angrier with every second that passed.

"What's wrong?" I asked.

"That asshole! He ditched again."

"Who ditched?"

"Vulkazir, a demon the SF paid to keep watch over my dragons when I'm not here, but that fucker ditched his post for the second time."

I took a step back when one of the dragons raised its head and bent down to place his reptilian-looking snout against the mesh.

Xanthia slipped her hand through a hole in the netting and rubbed her palm against his cheek. He leaned into it, his eyes closing. She crooned to him, and some of the tense anger eased from her shoulders.

I marveled at the size of the creature. The dragon's head was the size of a small car. Its body was easily the size of a small house. Slick leathery wings folded to its sides, but when Daniel and I approached, the dragon reared.

"I wouldn't get too close if I were you," Xanthia warned.

Daniel yanked me out of the way just as fire erupted from the dragon's mouth. If he hadn't jerked me back, the dragon fire would have fried me.

"Told you so," Xanthia replied. "Just give me a minute. I want to make sure they're all here."

I took a few more steps back. "You said they're babies? But they're so big."

Xanthia unlocked something around the corral. "Roofessee here is a Magnus Dragarion. That's why he's so big. But you see that one over there?" She pointed at a smaller dark-purple dragon that was the size of a horse. "That's the size of most baby dragons."

Once inside, she dashed around the pen, greeting each dragon as she went. All of them acted similarly to the first. They dipped their heads, seemed to be happy that she was there, and showed no aggression whatsoever.

Several times, however, the dragons nipped or spewed fire at one another. I yelped in fright when one of the dragons' fire shot right in front of Xanthia. However, she walked right through it, completely unaffected and emerged on the other side as if she were strolling in the park. Even her clothes remained intact.

"She really is resistant to fire."

Daniel nodded. "It is the reason she is a dragon trainer. Her father is one of the few demons breeds that are not susceptible to dragon fire. Most demons are. That chikabon in the battle would have burned if that fire had landed on him."

"But how come her clothes didn't burn?"

"I have heard of some half demons commissioning witches to have their demon strength woven into their clothing. A magical spell, so to speak, that keeps their clothes intact. Perhaps Xanthia has also done that."

When Xanthia joined us again, anger sparkled in her eyes. "I'm still only missing Quaneely, but a few of them have chain marks around their necks, which means someone recently tried to steal them." She exited the corral, locking it up behind her. "I'm going to kill Vulkazir when I find him!"

"And Quaneely is who you think killed the SF members on earth?" I asked.

"Yeah, she disappeared a few weeks ago, which was why Logan and his squad were called in to help. She's one of the younger Magnus Dragarions, only a year old, but my other two of that breed are still here. But those marks around their necks show that someone tried to take them, too, while I was gone." She finished locking up, her movements agitated. "I hope my babies burned whoever tried to steal them."

"So what do we do now that Vulkazir ditched his post? I mean, if no one's keeping an eye on them, what if whoever tried to steal them comes back?" I asked.

Xanthia seethed. "I'll talk to Logan when we get back. He was the one who suggested we commission a demon to guard their cage, but Vulkazir's the third demon to ditch his post. Fucking demons. You can't trust any of them."

"What about the other half demons in the SF." My breathing turned labored again as we climbed the hill. "Could one of them guard the dragons?"

Xanthia shook her head. "They can't withstand dragon fire so they would have to keep their distance, and there are so few half demons on SF payroll that I don't think Wes would risk it. Too many fuckers down here would try to take them out. None of them have the protection I do."

I huffed in the hot air as we climbed the hill away from the corral. "Are there other dragon trainers? Is it possible that dragons have been stolen from somewhere else too?"

Xanthia shook her head. "There are only three of us, but the other two aren't working right now. All of the dragons currently in training are right here."

"So few?"

She shrugged. "They don't breed often, only once a century."

I grumbled. "What about the adult dragons? Could they have tried to steal them as well?"

Daniel and Xanthia exchanged horrified looks.

Xanthia turned back to me. "Nobody, and I mean *nobody*, would mess with a full-grown guardian dragon. Besides, Lucifer wouldn't allow it. He would know immediately if one of his gates wasn't guarded. I would have heard about it. Hell, *everybody* would have heard about it." She shook her head. "It's safe to say that the only dragons possible of being stolen are my babies."

I nodded, starting to understand just how big of a deal it was to steal a dragon. "So they only have one dragon at the moment if they took Quaneely. That's good to know, but who's to say they won't come back and try again with the others."

"Exactly," Xanthia replied. "As soon as we finish this job, and after I give Wes my report, I'm coming back and staying here. I'm not risking the chance of any of my other dragons being stolen. I'll have to leave it up to Logan and his squad to track down Quaneely on earth." She snickered. "Cause, eventually, they'll find her. Wolves are the best trackers."

A faint smile graced my lips when I thought of Logan.

"And now we find a high-ranking demon?" Daniel arched a smooth eyebrow as his wings rippled. "Time is of the essence, and I fear our time here is growing increasingly long."

I shifted my thoughts from Logan back to the job at hand, but despite my angel powers flowing freely through me, a sense of unease filled me again. It didn't help that the longer we were in hell, the tenser Daniel was becoming.

Xanthia's mouth thinned into a tight line. "You bet your ass we do, cause until we find out who's behind this, all of my dragons are at risk."

Chapter 16

"Stay down and do exactly as I say," Xanthia whispered. "Trust me. You don't want to draw attention to yourself here."

I lay close to Xanthia's side on the burning ground at the top of a large hill, the sweltering heat singeing my clothes as we peered down. I couldn't believe what I was seeing. Tall black gates rose in a circle around what could only be described as a gladiator ring.

Inside, huge demonic creatures patrolled the perimeter as naked humans raced about the interior. The humans' panic and pain were evident in each bloodcurdling scream.

Several rows of stadium-like seats encircled the arena, on the outside of the gate but high enough up that they rose above the fenced perimeter. Dozens of different demon species sat on the benches, watching the bloodbath while cheering and stomping their feet.

I squeezed my eyes shut a few times. The humans, obviously souls that had been damned, were being slaughtered one by one. Several creatures, which Xanthia had explained weren't demons but underworld animals, chased the humans and killed them off.

As soon as the humans had all been killed, the perimeter demons scooped them into a big pile and disappeared into a cave below. When they reemerged, they dragged another dozen humans—fresh meat. All of the humans shook with fear.

Then the entire game started again.

But the humans' deaths weren't quick. The doglike animals, which looked as big as horses and had thickly muscled shoulders, low haunches, and jagged black teeth, took a bite out of each person as they ran by, seeming to enjoy making the process as painful as possible.

"What is this place?" I whispered.

"One of many arenas that the demons frequent on their days off," Xanthia replied.

Daniel's jaw locked. "And not a place I care to stay at long."

I gulped, squeezing my eyes shut again when one of the doglike creatures bit off the arm of a wailing human. "But I don't understand. They're killing the humans, so where do their souls go if they've already died on earth?"

"They're not really killed." Xanthia continued to keep her voice low. "They may look like they die, but in a few hours, their bodies will regenerate and be revived again. Then the whole process starts over. This particular batch of humans will probably spend several weeks here, doing these exact games over and over and over again before the demons return them to the gates of hell."

I shuddered, bile rising in the back of my throat.

"Is that him over there?" Daniel nodded toward the end of the stadium, where a particularly large demon sat on a throne.

Two large horns rose on his head like a bull's, but his black body reminded me of an insect, his legs and arms long and spindly. The pincers on the end of his arms looked razor-sharp and deadly.

Smaller demons ran back and forth between him and something in the back. They appeared to be bringing him drinks and things to eat. Blood dripped from the raw meat and random human body parts that appeared on their food trays. The demon threw each tray of food in his mouth, swallowing everything whole.

Xanthia tensed. "Yep, that's him. I figured he would be here."

"Who is he?" I asked.

"Rigarion. He's one of the highest-ranking demons in hell, a step below Lucifer. If anybody knows what's going on with my dragons and the demon possessions on earth, it will be him."

"So how may we assist you?" Daniel asked.

Xanthia flattened more to the ground, turning our way. "I want to have you as backup. I'm going to try approaching him myself, but if shit hits the fan, and I need to get out of there pronto, I'm gonna need both of you to help. The nearest portal is half a mile away. We'll literally have to run like hell to get there."

"If needed, I can carry both of you. I can fly us there," Daniel replied.

Xanthia snickered. "I forgot about those wings of yours. They may come in handy. Okay, we're gonna ease down this hill and circle around to where Rigarion is sitting. It's important that both of you stay exactly where I tell you. If things start to go bad, you may need to stop them from killing me."

I shook my head. "But I thought you had Lucifer's protection. How can they kill you?"

"Technically, I do have his protection, but asking any high-ranking demon for information or a favor doesn't usually go over well. Some take offense and throw caution to the wind. It wouldn't be the first time a half demon protected by Lucifer had been obliterated for overstepping his or her boundaries."

My mouth snapped closed. "Okay, Daniel and I will be ready, won't we?"

He gave a slight nod. "As you wish."

We slunk back down the hill, moving quickly and covertly behind the boulders. At the bottom, we circled around to the other side, the hot, fiery air filling my lungs.

The longer we'd been in hell, the harder it had become to breathe. I didn't know if that was from my anxiety over what we were doing or if all angels eventually felt that way in the underworld. Regardless, I didn't want to stick around to find out.

"Okay, keep your eyes open," Xanthia said as we crouched behind a large boulder. The stadium was directly in front of us, but Rigarion's back was to us. He couldn't be more than thirty yards away, yet his huge size had me biting my lip.

"We will, and be careful," I replied.

"Yes. God speed." Daniel's jaw clenched tighter.

Seeing Daniel so tense made my frown deepen. If I was starting to feel the effects of hell despite my half angel blood, I wondered if the effects on him were even stronger. It was quickly becoming apparent that we weren't completely immune to the environment in the underworld.

Xanthia emerged from around the boulder, and Daniel and I peeked out to watch. She approached the stadium confidently, a swagger in her hips. I knew it was all for show. I'd seen the stark fear in her eyes right before she took off.

It didn't take her long to reach the stadium. She already had her lasso out, coiled tightly in her hand. With a flick of her wrist, she would have it free, but at the moment, it appeared she had it hidden, on hand for necessary use only.

Sweat trailed down my temple. I wiped it away, frowning. That was the first indication of my body responding to the heat. A few beads of sweat also dotted Daniel's brow, but his attention stayed on Xanthia.

I watched my friend as she approached one of the minions serving Rigarion. Though I couldn't hear what they said, I gathered from the minion's shaking head that he was denying her.

Xanthia took a step toward him, extracting something from her pocket. It took me a minute to realize she was bribing him.

He bowed deeply and ushered her toward Rigarion. My breath caught in my throat as I waited to see the high-ranking demon's response.

Considering Rigarion faced the arena, it wasn't like we could read his expression—not that I would have known how to read a demon's expression—but given Daniel's tightly balled fists, I knew he also didn't like the unpredictability of what could happen.

Xanthia kept her head down, not looking Rigarion directly in the eye. After they exchanged a few words, she slowly extracted something else from her pocket.

When she showed it to him, he tipped back his head and laughed. The sound was loud enough that it rose above the fighting and screams from the arena.

Abruptly, Rigarion's head came crashing back down, and he swept his arm out in front of him, knocking Xanthia off her feet. He jumped up, standing over her and towering to his impressive and terrifying height.

Daniel and I both straightened, ready to rush to her aid, but a quick shake of Xanthia's head in our direction had us staying put.

Rigarion yelled a few things to his minions, none of which I understood. As they scrambled about, they clawed the air and gnashed their teeth.

Xanthia managed to stand back up as Rigarion continued to loom over her. She seemed to be pleading with him to tell her what we needed to know, but just when he raised his hand to strike her again, his movements paused.

He lifted his head, sniffing the sweltering air.

Xanthia's eyes widened, and she waved her arms, trying to catch his attention again, but he swung around, his glowing red eyes darting back and forth.

I gasped, and Daniel gritted his teeth.

Xanthia again tried to catch the demon's attention, but Rigarion continued to search the outer area. My breath sucked in when his head dropped, his gaze narrowing toward the boulder that Daniel and I hid behind.

With a giant leap, he catapulted over the arena and landed on the ground only twenty feet away. The force with which he hit the rocky ground made it rumble.

Xanthia sprinted from the stadium, several minions following her. "Please! Please, I can pay you! All I need is the name of the demon or supernatural behind this all."

The demon swung toward her, smoke puffing from his nostrils. "You lied to me, dragon trainer. You told me you were here alone." His voice trembled, deep and gravelly. I shivered.

"I . . . I am alone. Really, I swear."

Rigarion's attention swung back toward us. Daniel and I snatched our heads back around the boulder, my eyes widening as I realized he may have seen our movements.

"You lie, dragon trainer!" The demon's deep voice made goose bumps break out across my skin.

"Prepare to flee, young angel," Daniel whispered. "I could handle Rigarion in battle if he were alone, but with his minions also flanking him, I do not know if I will be the victor. I will fly you out of here. We must go."

I grabbed Daniel's hand. "No! We can't leave Xanthia. He'll kill her!"

Daniel's jaw locked. "I don't know if I can save you both."

"I'm not leaving her!"

The ground gave another violent shake, and before I could fully comprehend what was happening, Rigarion loomed above us.

I yelped. *Shit! Shit! Shit!* My powers rattled violently, shooting through my bloodstream like electric lasers.

"One of my minions told me an angel had decided to visit the underworld." His leathery lips lifted into a grotesque smile. "But he didn't tell me there was also a half human who still had her soul who accompanied the angel. I see that it's my lucky day."

Xanthia ran around the boulder's corner, panting. "Please, Rigarion! Leave them alone and let me pay you!"

Rigarion swung his large head her way. "You lied. You traveled here with both of them." His pincers snapped as more smoke flew from his nostrils. "And I don't care for your initial offer of payment, but perhaps we can reach another bargain."

Xanthia's mouth parted. "You won't take the tokens? But these will pay for over a thousand minions—"

Rigarion swung his arm, striking Xanthia's hand. The tokens she carried flew into the air. When they landed, the minions scrambled to pick them up.

Whatever payment Xanthia had held, she'd now lost.

"I don't want tokens! I want her soul!" He pointed at me and lifted his head, sniffing the air again. "I haven't smelled a soul that pure in centuries. A delicacy like no other." His tongue slithered out to lick his lips again.

With a start, I realized what had attracted Rigarion's attention. It hadn't been Daniel's and my movements. It had been my *scent*. My hybrid aroma, that Logan claimed made me smell like blooming roses, apparently was detectable by demons too.

Rigarion pointed a curling pincer directly at me. "If I can have her, you will get your information. But that is the only way you will walk free."

Chapter 17

Daniel was instantly on his feet, his wings extending wide. He scooped me into his arms and bent his knees. But just as he was about to fly, Rigarion smacked us aside as if we were bowling pins.

I screamed, the sound blending in with the horrific yells emitting from the arena.

Daniel landed hard on the fiery ground beside me, a loud grunt escaping him. A lock of hair fell across his forehead, and black coal smudged his cheeks.

A moment of hysteria rose within me. It was the first time I'd ever seen the angel dirty.

Xanthia leaped in front of us, her lasso out, the glowing rope emitting sparks. "She's not part of the bargain."

Rigarion laughed as his minions encircled us. A lump lodged in my throat, like a giant egg I couldn't swallow.

We were trapped.

Daniel and I stood just as the ground trembled again. Horror swam through me when a herd of chikabons crested the hill, running toward us on their hooved feet.

The color drained from Xanthia's face. Her arm fell, her lasso no longer positioned to strike.

Daniel hauled me against him. "Hold on to me, young angel. We must get out of here. Now!"

He once again spread his wings wide, but Rigarion sprang into the air, moving impossibly fast. He jumped on top of us, his alien-like black body crashing into my ribs with enough force to break them. I screamed as the stench of sulfur and rot filled my nose.

Gagging, I tried to scramble out from beneath him. The demon's heat scorched my skin, yet amazingly, I didn't burn.

My powers vibrated, catapulting to the surface and skimming across it like lightning on water. Instinctively, I raised my hands. Daniel did the same. We pressed our palms against the demon, red light emitting from our bodies.

Rigarion shrieked when we blasted him off us. He flew through the air, landing a dozen yards away.

"Are you all right?" Daniel asked, gasping.

I nodded tightly. "Is he dead?"

Xanthia crouched beside us, her panic-filled eyes watching the chikabons that had caged us in as if they were spectators at the bloody arena.

"No," she replied. "He's far from dead."

With wide eyes, I watched Rigarion rise to his feet, his insect-like mouth snapping as fire rolled in his throat.

Daniel and I jumped to our feet. He swept me behind him before prowling forward, his attention focused solely on the powerful demon.

The two of them circled each other, both crouched low, ready to strike.

"Daniel, no!" I cried, lunging forward.

But Xanthia grabbed my arm and hauled me back before I could intervene. "Don't, Dar! You can't stop them. It will just get you killed."

My heart thumped wildly. I already knew who the victor of the battle would be. As strong as Daniel was, he was one against hundreds. Rigarion's minions already cackled around us, rising to the balls of their feet, just waiting for the opportunity to strike. Their loud chatter filled the air, like hundreds of snapping insects about to devour their prey.

They wouldn't play fair as their demon lord battled an angel. They would pounce the second there was an opening, striking Daniel down when his back was to them.

Daniel circled in front of me again, his attention still on the demon. And in that moment, I knew what I needed to do.

I sprang forward and positioned myself between the dueling divine creatures. Rigarion's eyes glowed ruby red, his giant maw opening with delight.

"What is it that you want from me?" I seethed.

Daniel stopped, his turquoise eyes blazing. "No, Daria!"

Rigarion stepped closer to me, his head dipping until he looked at me at eye level. "Didn't I make myself clear, half human? You have a human soul, and given your angel heritage, that soul will be mouthwatering. Like nothing I've consumed before."

My skin glowed brighter, and power vibrated through me.

"I want you," he continued in his deep, gravelly voice. "If I can have you, your friends will walk free."

My nostrils flared. "We can get you more money. How much do you want for the information?"

His lips thinned, and he hissed, a horrible smoky sound projecting from his throat. "Listen closely, half human. This is your last chance. I want *you* and you alone. Only that will guarantee your friends will walk free with the information the dragon trainer requests."

"No," Daniel bellowed.

But I held up my hand, stopping him from advancing. The chikabons still stood on standby, while Rigarion's minions continued to chatter. With so many of them waiting to attack . . .

There was no way out.

I closed my eyes, picturing Logan's face and how he'd react if anything happened to me. The thought of him made my powers strengthen even more. They hummed and swirled, dipping through my body like blazing meteors.

Licking my parched lips, I remembered Daniel's

training. *It's imperative that when we step into hell, you don't fight your natural instincts. Those instincts are what will keep you alive.*

I raised my gaze to meet the demon's. "Okay, Rigarion, you have a deal. Tell Xanthia what she wants to know, and then let them go. If you do that, you can have me freely. We won't fight you."

"No, Dar!" Xanthia yelled.

Rigarion laughed. "What makes you think I can't take you now? You are three against hundreds."

"True. You outnumber us, but a full-blooded angel can kill you. Who's to say he won't kill you before you catch me, even if your minions try to help?"

Rigarion's pincers snapped together. He studied me, his blood-red eyes like coals while his sulfurous stench made me want to gag. "Fine," he finally roared. "You have a deal."

I sought out Daniel. His face had gone pale. I tried to convey confidence with my expression, but inside, I shook like a leaf. Still, I knew stopping Daniel and Rigarion's impending fight was the only way we stood any chance of escaping hell alive.

I swung back to the demon. "Tell your minions and the chikabons to leave. I won't willingly give myself to you until they're gone and my friends are free, and you *must* tell Xanthia who she seeks."

Rigarion dipped his head and barked something in an ancient tongue. The chikabons and the minions backed away, hissing and snapping their teeth, obviously disappointed they wouldn't be part of a bloodbath.

The demon whipped his head around to face Xanthia.

"A sorcerer by the name of Stephen Price has invented a portal that allows low-ranking demons and dragons to enter earth. That is who you seek."

"How do I know you're not lying?" My fingers curled into my palms, my skin glowing brightly.

"You don't, but it just so happens today's your lucky day. I do not lie."

I didn't know if we could trust him, but everything in the underworld seemed to be a gamble. However, Stephen did start with an *S*, and that was whom Jayden had referred to all those weeks ago. And as Xanthia had said, the demons were always trying to outrank each other. It would also serve in Rigarion's best interest if the demon helping Stephen Price was found out and removed.

I glanced at my half-demon friend. She seemed to have reached the same conclusion as me, yet terror still filled her eyes.

Daniel took Xanthia's arm, pulling her away. She fought and dragged her feet, but the angel was too strong. She couldn't break free.

When I was alone with Rigarion in the rocky field, his minions and the chikabons back at the arena, he took a step closer to me. "Don't try to run, half human. You won't make it far. If you submit easily, I will make this less painful."

"Why do I have the feeling that this time you *are* lying?"

He laughed, still advancing.

Tingles raced down my spine with each step that

brought him closer to me. My powers vibrated so strongly that I could barely tell where they ended and I began.

Trust yourself.

My heart beat like a jackhammer, and sweat dripped past my ear. I prayed for my angel instincts to take control and tell me what to do.

"Oh, half human, I can smell your fear. It's quite . . . delectable." Rigarion's leathery pincer encircled my waist, his body heat scorching my skin.

My lips parted, revulsion sweeping through me when a distant, whispery voice breezed across my mind.

Wait.

I jolted. It was the same voice that had appeared in my mind when my dark power had been born during the rogues' attack.

Hello? Who's there? I called frantically in my mind.

But the voice ignored my questions. *Daria. Wait.*

My jaw dropped and relief filled me that, even if I was hallucinating, I didn't feel alone. And strangely, for the first time, I recognized that the voice sounded like a *man*.

But I didn't have time to process that as the feel of Rigarion's hot breath slid over my cheek. He lifted me from the ground. Hot saliva dripped onto my arm.

"I've never smelled anything so delicious before. Your blood will be like honey."

A wave of disgust made me shudder. Rigarion's mouth opened. Fire swirled in the back of his throat.

Wait, the whispery voice said again.

My heart rate increased. *Seriously? I should wait?*

Rigarion's gaping maw spread wide. Breath that smelled of death, blood, and rot blew across my skin.

But before I could seek the voice again, Rigarion plunged me into his mouth, the fire from his throat scorching my skin.

In the distance, Xanthia yelled, "No!" and I feared it would be the last word I ever heard.

Chapter 18

Fire consumed my skin as Rigarion's mouth closed around me.

I was trapped—inside him.

There was no getting out.

"Daniel!" I screamed, but it was too late. Nobody could save me.

Rigarion's hot, leathery tongue moved me to the side of his mouth, like a giant snake propelling me around. His gigantic jaws could have crushed the length of my body with one bite.

My powers flowed so strongly within me that I almost couldn't control them, but I forced myself not to react. I closed my eyes. *Hello? Are you there? Please help me!*

Rigarion's tongue positioned me between his razor-sharp teeth.

Hello? I screamed.

Wait.

I cried in relief when the voice came in my mind again, but that relief vanished when pain needled my back. Just the contact with Rigarion's teeth had broken the skin along my spine. My blood trickled into his mouth, and a deep shudder ran through the demon.

I waited for my bones to crush and my tendons to snap.

But all Rigarion did was break my skin more, just enough for another trickle of my blood to enter his mouth.

Another deep shudder ran through him.

Bile rose in the back of my throat as comprehension dawned.

He was *savoring* me. He hadn't bitten down intentionally, as he planned to eat me slowly.

What do I do? I screamed in my mind. Panic welled up inside me as my powers vibrated violently along my skin, wanting out. Demanding that I let them out.

No, the voice commanded. *Not yet. Slide down his throat. Grasp his heart.*

Relief and revulsion swept through me simultaneously. I wasn't alone, yet what the voice demanded I do . . .

Another needlelike tooth penetrated my skin. More blood seeped from my body. I muffled a scream as a third deep shudder ran through Rigarion's body.

Now! the voice commanded.

Kicking against the demon's leathery tongue, I pushed myself deeper into the back of Rigarion's mouth and down his throat. Pain raked across my body as another tooth gouged my skin.

I swallowed a scream as I slid toward the fire that filled his belly.

Heat.

Pain.

Scorching heat.

Constriction.

I closed my eyes tightly. My skin felt on fire as his throat closed around me, squeezing me, breaking me.

Suffocating me.

I can't breathe!

I kicked harder, plunging deeper down his throat head first. Rigarion gagged, trying to expel me back into his mouth.

The air disappeared. Fire filled my surroundings.

No air.

There was no air!

A deep, throbbing beat reached my ears. Overwhelming heat enveloped me as I struggled to stay conscious.

No air!

Lub-dub. Lub-dub.

His heart. I could hear his beating heart.

Grab it! The instruction billowed to the forefront of my mind as my lungs constricted. I needed to get air!

Through his throat, into his chest. Grab it now!

I sucked in the last bit of air I could find and followed

the command, shoving my hand through the sticky flesh of Rigarion's throat as my dark power burned a hole through him.

Rigarion's scream rose around me, the sound everywhere as he shrieked and gagged.

My hand wrapped around something gelatinous and cold. Surprisingly cold. His heart pumped between my fingers as his throat constricted more.

My grip loosened. *Can't do it.*

I writhed and turned. His throat was too tight.

I can't breathe!

But the voice held firm. *Squeeze his heart now, and blast him with your power!*

Dizziness swam through my mind. There was no air.

No air.

No air.

Now! the voice bellowed.

I concentrated solely on the feel of Rigarion's cold, slippery heart as blackness closed around my mind. Squeezing harder, I mentally screamed in agony as energy shot from my fingertips, exploding into Rigarion.

Rigarion howled in pain as his body convulsed.

No air.

No air.

The gelatinous, rubbery heart detonated into pulverized mush.

All at once, the pressure released. A thousand lumps of flesh exploded around me. I flew from the demon as his body turned to ash.

I catapulted through the air, sucking in deep breaths

of heat and sulfurous air. I screamed as my body twisted and flew.

"Umph!" I landed hard.

My body crumpled to the ground as the wind was knocked out of me. Hot smoke and fire rose from the ground. I choked and coughed, gasping.

My mind reeled. *I made it out of him alive!*

My throat tightened as more gasping breaths consumed me, but the dizziness and blackness in my mind faded.

I frantically searched for Rigarion, but all that was left of the demon was a mountain of ash. My hands flew to my body, and I felt for injuries.

Blood caked my shirt, making it stick to my back. My fingers shook when I saw the black gelatinous stains running down my hands, but I didn't have time to dwell on it. The ground vibrated, shaking me.

With wide eyes, I scrambled clumsily to my feet as the minions and the chikabons, who'd retreated to the arena, came galloping toward me.

I staggered, trying to run.

"Xanthia! Daniel!" I screamed for my friends, but my voice came out in a hoarse whisper.

Run! The voice commanded.

I turned and sprinted.

The minions and chikabons were already advancing. The only chance I had was to run as fast as I could toward the portal.

My legs moved stiffly, like a broken dancer. The ground rumbled more, the sounds of a hundred screams rising behind me. But they weren't screams from the humans. They were screams from the devil's army.

And they were closing in on me.

Hot scorching air filled my lungs as I ran and ran, my shoes slapping against the dark hot ground. I didn't look over my shoulder for fear of what I would see, but I knew the chikabons and minions were gaining ground. I could feel their energy and smell the stench of their rotting bodies.

I searched again for Daniel and Xanthia in the black rocky terrain. They couldn't have gone far. I knew they wouldn't have left me, but geysers of spouting fire and intermittent gusts of ashy smoke made it impossible to see. I didn't even know if I was running the right way.

Panic rose in my throat just as a rush of air whooshed against my back. I shrieked and dared a look over my shoulder, only to have my eyes widen with horror. Three chikabons were hot on my tail, only yards away.

I stumbled over a rock and almost fell but righted myself at the last moment.

Where are they?

I frantically leaped over a crevice. Just as I went airborne, a chikabon slashed against my back.

I screamed in agony and fell forward, knocking the wind out of me again. *No!*

When I flipped around, demons leaned over me. I brought my hands up to cover my face. My powers rushed up again. I didn't know if I could beat them all, but I would die trying.

One of the chikabons opened its mouth to bite, but a

blast of fire shot over my body, like someone spraying napalm. It lit the three chikabons on fire.

A roar like I'd never heard before came next, followed by more blasts of fire. The heat from the blasts was hotter than anything I'd felt in hell, as if my skin could melt right off.

Scrambling away from the fire, I looked up.

Huge leathery wings brushed air against my cheeks as a dragon flew above me. My eyes widened in shock as its scaly belly filled my vision. It couldn't have been more than fifteen feet away. The dragon flew low to the ground, incinerating every demon in its path.

I sat up, disbelief coursing through me that a creature from hell was protecting me, but then I caught a glimpse of the figure astride the dragon's giant back.

Xanthia's long black hair flew behind her as she commanded the dragon. She rode him over the field, her dragon's fire destroying all of the minions and chikabons.

The stench of burning flesh and sulfur was so strong that I choked. But the fires just rose higher. The field I'd run from only moments ago burned with blistering heat as screaming minions and chikabons writhed in its grasp. The smoke and ash caused tears to sting my eyes. I coughed, trying to gulp in more air.

Another thump came from beside me. I brought my hands up, ready to blast my dark power into whatever demon had found me, but instead, I cried in relief.

Daniel crouched down, his huge white wings stretched and ready for him to ascend. His strong arms slipped under my knees and around my ragged back. I hissed in pain, but it didn't stop his smile. "Well done, young angel."

He lifted me from the ground and launched us into the air. Xanthia continued to circle around behind us, her dragon breathing lines of fire along its path, stopping any demon that tried to reach us.

"Where's the portal?" I clung to Daniel as we flew through a mountain of billowy smoke. Ash and sulfurous stench filled my nose.

"Just ahead."

"What about Xanthia?"

"She's coming."

We landed on the ground a moment later. My teeth chattered from the force, but a burst of hope shot through me when I saw the shimmering black-and-silver portal only yards away.

Daniel set me back on my feet, but I struggled to stand. My brush with death had left me weak and more shaken than I'd realized.

"Stay strong, young angel."

I forced my trembles to stop just as another huge rumble almost shook me off my feet.

Xanthia's dragon landed in front of us, its immense weight making the ground vibrate. My breath caught at the sight. The huge dragon lifted his wings and flapped them twice before settling them next to his body. He laid his huge head on the ground, and Xanthia slid off his neck before crooning something into his ear.

He rubbed his enormous cheek against her, his eyes closing briefly when their skin made contact. She said something else to him before stepping back.

The dragon rose again, and with an awkward step to the left, his immense wings stretched as he took off at a lumbering run. But when his massive wings extended and he lifted into the sky, his body was nothing but beauty and grace.

For a moment, I just stared. Of all of the creatures I'd seen in hell, only the dragons were beautiful.

"Come on. Let's go!" Xanthia grabbed my arm and pulled me toward the portal. "That won't be the end of them!"

Daniel grabbed my other hand, and the three of us raced to the portal door. We leaped through it, the dark void sucking us in, and the depths of hell disappeared behind us.

Chapter 19

We emerged in the McDonald's parking lot, the portal spitting us out like coughed-up food.

I landed on all fours on the hard pavement. A puddle of dirty rainwater stared back at me. Above, the stars and moon shone.

The only good thing about the transfer back was that it didn't take as long as the first, and we all emerged at the same time.

"We made it!" Xanthia dusted her arms off. "And good thing Rigarion is dead. If he weren't, the next time I traveled back to hell, that fucker would have annihilated me."

An excited gleam still coated her eyes. At least one of us had enjoyed delving into the underworld.

Daniel straightened his shirt. "Yes, agreed."

I stayed as I was, gulping in deep breaths, yet I couldn't help but notice that neither Xanthia nor Daniel had fallen over.

I rolled my eyes. *Seriously, someday I will get good at this.*

As it was, I didn't mind the feel of the hard, gritty pavement beneath my palms. Everything about it felt familiar and safe—like home.

And it certainly beat the remnants of Rigarion that clung to my clothes and hair. Sticky goo and gelatinous bits of Rigarion's heart encrusted my fingers, but I still grinned.

We'd made it back to Earth. We'd survived hell, and we'd found out who was behind the attacks on the SF.

The fresh scent of ozone lingered in the air. It had rained recently. I inhaled deeply, never having smelled anything so good in my life. After a few more deep breaths, I pushed back onto my haunches.

But my grin abruptly faded when pain seared through me. I hissed just as Xanthia exclaimed, "Oh my god, Dar! Look at your back!"

She crouched at my side, her long hair falling in wild strands around her shoulders. "Does it hurt? You've got blood everywhere."

I grimaced. Stinging pain electrified the nerves in my back every time I moved. "Is it bad?" I glanced over my shoulder, trying to see the extent of the damage.

"Um, let's just say that Logan will not be happy when he sees that." Xanthia pushed herself up and held out her hand. "Want a hand up?" She made a face at how filthy I was, but her hand remained.

A refusal was on the tip of my tongue since I couldn't touch others, when something stirred within me. An awareness. A notice that something was . . . different about myself.

"Oh shit." Xanthia stuffed her hand into her pocket with a look of embarrassment. "Sorry, Dar. I forgot you can't touch people."

But I barely heard her. My heart beat harder with every second that passed.

I extended my arms, taking in the subtle glow of my angel powers coursing beneath my skin. For the first time since landing on earth, my powers felt free.

My heart beat harder.

Clumsily, I stood, the pain in my back forgotten. "Daniel! Look at my skin!"

Similar to how they'd been in Emunda and the underworld, my powers flowed freely and openly, the storage box I normally stored my light in gone. A subtle angelic hue lit up my skin, as if a soft glow lightbulb powered within my body.

Daniel's lips curved up. Once again, his beautiful dark locks appeared perfectly disheveled and tantalizingly soft. Any trace of the black dirt that had caked his clothing or skin in hell had disappeared.

"You've come into your powers." His smile stretched as he ran a finger along my arm. His touch did nothing out of the ordinary. It didn't push my powers down or diminish them, not like it had when they'd been raging out of control.

With how they felt, I no longer needed his help.

My grin returned as a deep sense of awareness filled me again. At the moment, my powers just . . . existed.

Daniel dropped his hand back to his side. "You did exactly as I told you to do when battling Rigarion. You followed your instincts and let your powers run free. And now, they exist within you as every angel's powers are meant to reside. You've finally mastered what I've been training you for. Well done, young angel!" Pride filled his voice.

A feeling of giddiness rose inside me. "So I'm . . . what? I'm cured or whatever you want to call it?"

Daniel laughed, the sound rich and deep. "You're still young, Daria Gresham. Your powers may continue to grow, but you've mastered the elementary training. You've learned how to exist with your powers as they flow freely within you. Tell me, young angel, how does your light feel?"

I closed my eyes and concentrated on my powers. "My light feels . . ." I cocked my head. My light no longer resided below my navel, and my dark no longer tried to dominate my light.

Instead, what had once felt like two separate life forces in my womb, felt like radiant energy and cool power flowing simultaneously through my veins. Each power was distinguishable if I focused on them hard enough, but they no longer felt like completely separate beings, and they no longer rushed eagerly to the surface, trying to break free.

It was like everything had . . . clicked.

My breath came out in a rush when I opened my eyes. "My light feels free, and it's moving with my dark. I don't feel like I need to push them down anymore."

Daniel nodded. "And that is how they should feel. Tell me, what do you feel when you touch Xanthia?"

Xanthia raised an eyebrow. "Whoa, bro. I'm half demon, remember? I don't really want her to blow me to bits."

"You're not full-blooded. Daria won't hurt you."

I stood still, excitement and fear warring within me. Was Daniel saying I could touch people? Not just potential mates, but . . . everyone?

My jaw dropped, my heart rate picking up. "Wait a minute, Daniel. Are you saying . . ."

My throat felt too thick for me to speak, so I took a few deep breaths again. When I finally felt like I could talk, I asked, "Are you saying I can touch *anyone?*"

"Yes. The way you controlled your powers previously, the way you locked your light away so it wouldn't hurt you unless you were around those potential mates your mother told you of . . . that is not how angelic power naturally works. Your family's way of dealing with your angel powers perverted it. Angels can touch anyone. Our purpose is to heal and banish evil. And when our powers are allowed to function naturally, touch doesn't inhibit us. You should be able to touch freely now."

Xanthia's eyebrows rose, a look of unease settling upon her face despite Daniel's words. I couldn't blame her. She'd just watched me be swallowed by a demon before I blew him up from the inside out. Yeah, I would be nervous too.

"Are you sure?" I wrung my hands, making a face when Rigarion's goo made them stick together.

Daniel gave me a placating smile. "I'm sure."

"Let's just get this over with." Xanthia held out her arm stiffly. "But try not to get all that gross stuff on me, and Daniel, you'd better put me back together if she kills me."

"Of course, Xanthia. However, my help shall not be needed."

"Okay, here goes nothing." As I reached toward her, my hand shook. Never had I been able to touch anyone normally, not really.

Even when I'd been a little girl, before I'd come into my witch magic and begun training my light—which I'd thought was part of my witch magic but was actually from my angel side—I'd still received tingles from people. They weren't as strong as when I was an adult, but still, it made hugging my mom and my nan somewhat uncomfortable, but they'd understood. They'd gone through the exact same thing.

Tears pooled in my eyes the closer my fingers got to Xanthia. If only my mom and my nan could see me. If only they'd discovered in their lifetimes that we were all half angels. If only they'd learned how to let their magic flow freely too.

If they had, we all could have lived among others without fear of touching them. Our lives would have been so different.

Less lonely.

Less reclusive.

I touched Xanthia's arm lightly and held my breath. Her eyes widened.

We both waited and watched.

When nothing happened—no jolts, no tingles, no painful shocks, only the feel of her smooth skin as my powers continued to flow languidly in my body—I laughed. "Holy crap! I'm touching you!"

Xanthia grinned, a relieved sigh escaping her. "And you haven't killed me! Yay for both of us!"

Her comment only made me laugh harder.

"But my skin still glows." I broke our contact and studied my forearms. A subtle glow rose from my flesh.

"You need to learn how to temper your powers. Then that will cease while you're upon earth." Daniel placed his muscled forearm beside mine. As usual, his tanned skin looked nothing but perfectly smooth, blemish-free, and without a trace of glow. Not to mention that none of hell's remnants stuck to *his* skin.

Show-off.

I shook my head. "How do you do that? Your skin looks like a human's."

"Feel your powers. They flow beneath our skin, yes, but they don't have to flow so closely to it. Temper them. Subtly pull the powers to live closer to your bones. Encourage them to burrow more into your muscles."

I frowned. "Burrow them into my muscles and ask them to stay by my bones. Right. Cause it's so easy."

Daniel chuckled. "You shall learn this too."

"When?"

"With practice."

"Um, speaking of your glow . . ." Xanthia cocked her head toward the McDonald's. A group of laughing teenagers pushed through the door. They didn't glance our way, and even if they had, the sorcerers' mind control spells meant they wouldn't have seen us anyway since we stood so close to the portal, but still . . .

"That may be a problem," Xanthia continued. "Ya know, cause people can see your glowing skin."

My stomach dropped. She was right. My skin glowed subtly in the nighttime, not as strongly as it did in Emunda but strong enough that it would draw attention—attention I didn't want.

My frown deepened. "So if I want to let my powers flow freely, and if I want to touch people, I basically need to be a hermit and never leave my house for fear of drawing attention, unless I can learn to temper my powers."

Daniel threaded his fingers through mine—not reacting when Rigarion's goo coated them—and pushed his power into me.

My powers tempered, and my glow disappeared. I once again looked human.

"I shall continue training you." He gave my hand a squeeze. "However, for a while, you may need to withdraw from public outings."

"Wonderful." I sighed heavily.

"Cheer up, Dar. You'll get the hang of it eventually, and speaking of being in public, should we get going?" Xanthia nodded toward the SF sedan. "You know, cause some dipshit sorcerer has stolen Quaneely and is encouraging low-level demons to invade earth. I'm thinking we should probably report that to Wes fairly soon."

I tightened my hold on Daniel, using his strength to temper my powers. It was weird. I could feel what he was doing, but I didn't know how to replicate it on my own.

Regardless, Xanthia was right. The importance of my not being able to venture to Starbucks anytime soon for coffee was negligible. A murdering sorcerer who seemed hell-bent on destroying the Supernatural Forces was on the loose. That was definitely a more pressing matter.

"Yeah, you're right. We need to head back." I rolled my shoulders, my back still stinging. "Do you mind healing me quickly, Daniel? Then we can be on our way."

He arched a perfectly sculpted eyebrow. "You do not need me to heal you. Your powers will do that."

"They will?"

"Of course. Angels can heal themselves."

My lips parted as I remembered how my werewolf bite had healed while I'd been unconscious.

Was that because I hadn't been shoving my light into its storage box while I'd been unconscious? Had it worked with the dark power to heal me? Or had the dark power done it on its own?

I faced Daniel squarely, dropping his hand. "So does the dark power heal me, or does my light? I could never heal myself before when I only had my light."

"Your light heals others, but to heal yourself, you need both working as one. Now, close your eyes and concentrate. Call upon your powers and heal yourself. Knit your skin back together. Purify your blood of any toxins. Working together, your powers will keep you healthy for many years to come."

I swallowed. "How many years?"

"That remains to be seen. You're half human. Therefore, you are mortal, but you are also half angel who's now existing as she rightfully should—unlike your ancestors—so it's possible your human life will be extended many years beyond what the other women in your family experienced."

"Sweet." Xanthia crossed her arms. "Logan will be happy about that since werewolves tend to outlive humans by a hundred years or so."

My excitement grew. *Logan and I could both live hundreds of years together?* But I pushed that startling realization aside and said to Daniel, "You mean my ancestors that had both their dark and light powers lived much longer than normal humans? And that's how long I'll live now?"

Daniel's turquoise eyes brightened. "Exactly. You mentioned that hundreds of years ago, your ancestors still had both of their powers. How long did *they* live? That is the true question you should be asking as that would most likely reflect how long *you'll* live."

I thought of Master Gregor and the psychic. It was possible that somewhere in the history books, more information about my family resided—information that could potentially give me the answers I so desperately craved.

I shook my head. I was getting off track. At the

moment, I needed to heal myself so we could return to headquarters and warn Wes about Stephen. But once that mess was all done and over . . .

Then I would seek answers about my past, and I would learn everything there was to know about my family's history.

Chapter 20

"That's it, Daria. You're doing wonderfully."

Daniel's soft encouragement penetrated my concentration as I crouched in the parking lot. Sweat beaded along my upper lip. I pushed my dark and light to my back, focusing on swirling it around my shredded skin.

But healing myself proved harder than I thought it would.

It didn't help that I'd only just learned how to let my powers flow simultaneously inside me, and healing myself was something I'd never done before.

Not while I was conscious, at least.

"You're thinking about this too much," Daniel said. "Let your angel powers work naturally, healing you from the inside out. Don't force it. Encourage but don't force."

I sighed, frustrated as hell that I couldn't figure it out quicker, but something he said stuck. *You're thinking about this too much.*

The one time I'd healed myself from a rogue werewolf bite had been after I'd accidentally blasted Phoenix with my dark power. I'd been unconscious when that healing had occurred. Obviously, I hadn't been thinking then at all.

"Let your powers be free, Daria. Angel magic doesn't need to be controlled. It's who we are. Let your powers do our maker's work."

I relaxed my shoulders completely and exhaled. Keeping my eyes closed, I softly encouraged my magic to flow more into my back. I didn't push it or try to control it. More or less, I gave it a subtle nudge, but that was it.

A tingling began in my back followed by a cooling sense of numbness. A shocked realization hit me that it didn't hurt. Healing other people *always* hurt. That was par for the course, but at the moment . . . only my back hurt where Rigarion had shredded my skin.

As I crouched completely still while letting my powers flow beneath my ragged skin, the stinging pain disappeared. The muscle aches vanished. I could actually *feel* my skin sewing back together.

"Holy shit," Xanthia whispered. "Look at her skin!"

"That's it, young angel." Daniel's voice was filled with pride.

When the tingles disappeared, I stood and spun in a circle, trying to see my back, but in reality, I probably resembled a dog chasing its tail.

"Am I healed?" I asked, coming to a stop.

Daniel grinned. "Completely."

I whooped while Xanthia merely blinked, looking like a deer caught in headlights. "I've never seen magic like that before. Your skin . . . it pulled back together right before my eyes."

Daniel's grin remained in place. "Angel powers, not magic."

Once Xanthia stopped gaping, we strode across the parking lot toward the SF car. Despite my back being healed, I was still a complete mess and in desperate need of a shower, but that would have to wait until after we spoke to Wes.

"At least Logan won't lose his shit now when he sees you." Xanthia nodded toward my back. "Although your shirt is still shredded and bloody. That looks kinda weird."

"And my skin still glows." I lifted my arm. I'd been hoping that since I'd been able to heal myself, that I would miraculously learn how to temper my powers, too, but no such luck. They still flowed freely inside me but too closely to my skin. It didn't appear that my angelic hue would be fading anytime soon.

Even though I didn't worry about my powers shooting out of me, I also knew I couldn't venture out in public anytime soon—at least, not the humans' public.

Daniel clasped my hand and pushed his power into me. As before, I felt it when he tempered my powers and pushed my light down, but I couldn't replicate it.

Ugh.

"Have no fear, young angel. One step at a time. And remember, you've made remarkable progress. With more training and practice, you, too, shall be able to temper yourself and reach the height of your angelic powers."

"So when I reach the height of my angel powers, does that mean I'll eventually sprout wings?" I wasn't sure how I'd hide those on earth, but it would be cool to fly.

Daniel chuckled. "Most likely not. I only know of full-blooded angels that have wings." When he saw my dejected expression, he added, "But you are proving to be a very curious angel. I suppose only time will tell if your powers develop to that extent. I have not, after all, been acquainted with any half-blood angels descended from archangels. You are the first."

"Wings . . . now that would be cool." Xanthia reached into her pocket and extracted the car keys.

Thankfully, our SF sedan hadn't been towed. Then again, who knew how long we'd been gone since time in the divine realms didn't adhere to earth hours. For all I knew, we'd only been gone ten minutes.

We slipped into the car, and Xanthia started the engine. When she peeled out of the parking lot, I looked behind me, getting a glimpse of my ripped and bloody shirt. I wrinkled my nose. My clothing reeked of rot and sulfur.

My shoulders slumped. Even though my injuries were healed, I was a sight. Unlike Daniel, I couldn't magically clean my clothes or my skin. Every inch of me looked like I'd gone to battle.

Speaking of Daniel's clothes...

I leaned forward, peering around the front seat to stare at him. His massive shoulders stretched his very tight T-shirt that had magically reappeared in the portal transfer. I distinctly remembered his previous shirt being shredded when his wings sprouted.

I groaned in frustration that I still had so much to learn and laid my head back against the headrest. Learning how to grow clothes during portal transfers was another thing we could add to things-Daria-still-needs-to-learn-in-training list.

But one thing was apparent—there was no way his shirt could hide wings beneath it.

"What happened to your wings?" I asked as Xanthia picked up speed. The car's headlights cut through the night, illuminating the quiet streets.

Daniel angled his body toward me. "They have retracted. I only call them forth when necessary."

"Could you call them forth now, while you're on earth and not in a divine realm?"

"I could, but I do not see why I would need to."

"Is going to war with a sorcerer, a stolen dragon, and who knows how many low-level demons that have possessed supernaturals a good enough reason?" Xanthia asked as she flicked on the vents. A cool rush of air flowed from the dash.

Daniel's mouth hardened, and a sense of uneasiness settled within me.

"It could be," he replied. "However, there has not been a battle between demons and angels on earth in many millennia, not since before the portal allowing demons to transfer from hell was sealed from earth."

Xanthia sped up as we cruised onto the interstate. Miles ahead of us, the foothills appeared in the moonlight.

Xanthia's expression turned grim. "Well, bro, let's hope history doesn't repeat itself."

Chapter 21

We passed my tour bus on the way back to headquarters. It still hovered on the side of the road not far from the magical barrier but far enough away that Mike's and Cecile's memories remained intact.

I straightened in my seat when Xanthia cruised past. The bus's dark windows stared back at us, so I knew Mike and Cece were asleep. Tomorrow I would find them and let them know I'd returned, but there was no point waking them at the moment.

However, I would eagerly wake up one person if needed.

My senses prickled in anticipation when our sedan approached the SF vehicle portal access door.

After Xanthia, Daniel, and I all scanned our palms,

Xanthia drove forward. She seemed unfazed by the strange sensation that billowed through the car when the portal door swallowed us whole.

When we emerged on the other side, the large SF garage waited.

Xanthia pulled forward and swung into an open spot. Two technicians bustled to us, one tall and lanky, the other short and stout. Each held a tablet and waited expectantly, ready for the identification processing.

"Xanthia Cummings, nice to see that you've returned in one piece." The stout SF technician scanned her wrist after we emerged from the vehicle.

The other one scanned me but kept his distance. I felt fairly certain my bloody, ripped clothing and gelatinous encrusted hands could be blamed for that. Not to mention, I smelled.

As before, when the technician tried to scan Daniel, the scanner couldn't identify Daniel's lineage.

"He's an angel," the other SF technician stated. "Wes already cleared him while the witches continue to work on a way to identify that breed."

That breed. Inside, I giggled. So far, the SF scanning devices had only identified me as a witch.

Xanthia put her hands on her hips after they finished admitting us. "How long were we gone?"

The technician checked his tablet. "Three days and four hours."

My eyebrows rose. Similar to Emunda, time passed differently in the underworld. Still, three days was a long time.

The lanky technician holstered his device. "We alerted Wes to your return while you were coming through the portal. He's called an emergency meeting among most of the squads and is on his way to the main command room right now. He told us you're to meet him there."

"Righty-o," she replied.

The three of us headed toward the door to the underground tunnel that led to the main building. As we pushed it open, Xanthia looked my frame up and down. "Do you want to shower first? There's a women's locker room in the back here. Changes of clothes are also available."

"Really? Do we have time?" The thought of a shower was almost as appealing as seeing Logan.

"If you're quick. Wes probably isn't in the command room quite yet, and since all of the squads are coming, I imagine a few are still rolling out of bed." She nodded toward the clock on the wall. It was just after two in the morning.

I rubbed my sticky fingers together. "A shower would be great, and I'll be fast. Promise."

After Xanthia showed me to the locker room, I took a hurried shower, but still had to shampoo my hair twice to get it fully clean. When I emerged, I felt like a new person.

Beside the shower, a tall shelf held neatly folded piles of blue soft-cotton pants and shirts in various sizes. They even had underwear and—hallelujah—sports bras.

I grabbed what I needed before chucking my ruined clothes and shoes in the garbage. Though I was thankful that I hadn't been wearing any of my favorite garments in hell, my heart tugged.

Replacing those clothes would cost money.

Money I didn't have.

With a final sigh, I slid on a pair of sturdy slip-ons provided by the SF and took a final look in the mirror. Wet hair hung down my back, but it was clean, and I smelled good. All in all, I felt a million times better.

Finally done, I joined Xanthia and Daniel in the hall. Xanthia anxiously paced, while Daniel stood serenely, as if he didn't have a care in the world.

"Ready?" Xanthia's eyes brightened when she saw me. She pulled her SF tablet from her pocket and bit her lip. "Wes just arrived in the command room. We better hurry."

She grabbed my hand and pulled me along, seeming to relish that she could actually touch me without fear of dying.

After a dizzying walk through the maze of tunnels and underground corridors, Xanthia stopped at a large door and took a deep breath before opening it.

My heart jumped into my throat when the room full of people waiting on the other side appeared. I scanned the area, looking for Logan, and spotted him on the far side.

My breath caught at the sight of him. He wore jeans and a T-shirt, and his toned hard body was outlined in every ripple of the soft cotton top. Mussed dark hair covered his head, as if he'd just rolled out of bed.

My skin tingled, and my lady parts tightened. *Damn,*

he's so sexy. Even though my angel powers existed as they should, my body still recognized him as a potential mate—if that could even explain my attraction to him. Maybe potential mates were truly just people that the women in my family were immensely attracted to and *that* was why our light never reacted to them.

Whatever the case, my attraction to Logan hadn't diminished in the slightest. Already, I envisioned my hands running all over his body.

Logan's eyes locked with mine, and a look of relief passed over his face before his head lifted subtly, and he sniffed.

Even across the room, he'd detected my arousal.

He crossed the distance between us in a blurred move, his werewolf gene kicking in.

Then he stood right in front of me.

Before he could blink, I threw my arms around his neck, his eyes widening in surprise at my uninhibited touch, but I didn't stop to explain.

Finally, I could touch him again, *feel* him—all of him, not just small little caresses or stolen kisses that didn't provoke my dark power.

But as soon as that realization came, so did a crashing understanding of what that meant. Reality landed on me like a million pounds of mud burying one in a landslide.

I wanted Logan, yet I could touch *anyone*.

But . . . I still only wanted Logan.

Any concern that what I felt for him was all a ruse of fated mates, all some trick of my family's magic, evaporated. If I could touch anyone, I could have sex with anyone in order to birth my sole daughter, but my heart only longed for Logan.

But what about Crystal?

I pushed that nagging thought away, not wanting to dwell on what the future held and tightened my hold on him.

"You're back, you're glowing, and you're *touching* me." A wild look filled his eyes, as if he were afraid I would disappear at any second. His eyes scanned over me as his heat warmed me from head to toe. "But how—"

My fingers threaded through the hair on the nape of his neck, and I longed to kiss him. "I learned how to control my powers. I mean *not* control them."

"So we can touch now?"

"Yeah." Tears filled my eyes. I reveled in the feel of his body against mine—his hard to my soft, his large build to my smaller one.

"But what changed?"

"I don't know how to explain it, but in the underworld, it was like something inside me clicked. Ever since we came back from hell, my powers have stayed flowing freely, and it feels good, like this is how I should have always been."

At that moment, everything I said was true. My powers felt normal. It seemed so simple to exist, yet years of bad habits, of trying to bury my light away, had been hard to break.

"It all happened when Rigarion—" I stopped midsentence. If Logan knew that a high-ranking demon had tried to eat me, he would probably go ape-shit. "Um, when something happened down there, I finally understood what Daniel had been telling me all along, to trust my instincts and let everything go—and it all clicked. I don't know how else to explain it."

Logan's eyes glowed as they swam with desire, relief, and something more. He trailed a finger along my cheek.

I sank into his touch. "It's like before now, when we first kissed above that rest stop, when I didn't have the dark power inside me. Except now I have both my powers and I can still touch—"

His mouth descended, crushing his lips to mine.

I opened to him, eagerly meeting his demanding kiss. In the back of my mind, I was vaguely aware that we stood in a room full of people, but at the moment, I didn't care.

Logan's tongue plunged into my mouth, dancing with my tongue. I sighed as a deep shudder of desire and relief coursed through me. My grip on his neck tightened when he leaned me back, arching me over his arm as he ravaged my mouth.

He tasted *so* good. Hell . . . he tasted *amazing*.

A hard bulge pressed into my abdomen, and a low moan escaped me, but then someone discreetly cleared their throat behind us.

Logan straightened, still holding me flush against his body. Damn, he was hard. So *hard*.

Wes looked down at me with raised eyebrows. I could have sworn he looked amused, but that look abruptly vanished when he said, "We'd like to start this meeting. Since you were present in the underworld, we'd appreciate your input, Daria. And Logan, if we're correctly able to identify whoever is behind the SF attacks, we'll be going after him—or her—tomorrow. Perhaps you should keep that in mind and focus on the meeting."

Logan set me back on my feet, but he held onto me until I regained my footing. "Of course, sir."

The entire room had grown quiet, and everyone stared at us. Only Alexander, Jake, Brodie, and Xanthia looked amused. The rest—at least twenty squads, each four to eight members—watched Logan and me with annoyed expressions.

Right. Perhaps holding up a meeting for which everyone was pulled from their beds wasn't a good idea.

"Sorry." I straightened more, carefully extracting myself from Logan's limbs.

His grip on me tightened before he reluctantly let go.

Somehow, I managed to sit down at one of the seats around the large table without blushing too hard, but I still caught a few snickers when Logan made a point to stay close to my side. Daniel pulled out the chair on my other side, and Xanthia took the chair beside him.

I rearranged my blue top and straightened my pants, but it was Chloe's and Priscilla's seething glares from across the table that stopped me short.

Their eyes shot daggers at me. Since I didn't see Phoenix with their squad, he must not have been healthy enough yet to join the meeting.

"So nice of you to join us." The saccharine tone made goose bumps rise on my skin as the chair beside Chloe was pulled out. My jaw dropped before I snapped it closed, my teeth grinding together when I saw *her*.

Holly, the drop-dead gorgeous cloaking-specialist witch—who'd mocked my mother's death, trailed her hand seductively over Logan, and whom I hadn't seen since Jayden's attack on me back in Silver City—smirked in my direction, her full lips glossy and ripe. She gave Logan a sultry smile. "Always nice to see you, too, Logan."

Logan merely nodded, barely paying her a passing glance.

Still . . .

Beneath my skin, my angel powers flared.

Apparently, they still responded to my emotions but not as volatilely. Thankfully, the dark power stayed calm, not like it would have a few days ago if I'd been confronted with three bitches, err, two witches and a fairy.

"Did you have fun in hell?" Holly twirled a lock of dyed-red hair around her finger. Considering she wore a full face of makeup and sported expertly curled hair, it was hard to believe she'd just rolled out of bed, or perhaps she was one of those women that always looked amazing no matter what time of day it was.

I smiled sweetly, my insides prickling. "It was lovely. Especially this time of year."

Xanthia laughed but quickly muffled it behind a cough.

Holly glared at me as Chloe and Priscilla whispered behind their hands.

I inwardly sighed.

I officially had three SF members against me. Never mind that I'd never done anything to Holly. I could understand Chloe and Priscilla's angst, but with Holly it seemed my being with Logan was enough to piss her off.

Daniel laid his hand on my thigh, pushing his calming powers into me. Some of his soothing, full-blooded angelic light flowed into my veins.

My very *human* anger, annoyance, and frustration calmed. I sighed. If only I were a full-blooded angel. Then I probably would never feel such unwanted and ungodly emotions.

Logan curled his hand around mine and squeezed, which effectively stopped any further wayward thoughts.

Wes sat down at the head of the table. "Shall we begin?"

Everyone nodded and murmured in agreement.

"Xanthia? Would you like to start?" Wes leaned forward, a keen interest in his eyes.

Xanthia straightened and tapped her tablet's screen. "Yes, sir. I've already written a concise brief of what happened in the underworld. All of you should have it in your inbox."

I raised my eyebrows. Daniel also cocked his head.

"When did you write that?" I asked quietly, leaning toward Xanthia while everyone pulled up the file.

Logan already had his tablet out, the brief open in front of him.

"When you were in the shower." Xanthia skimmed her finger along her tablet. "I dictated it since I knew Wes would want the report pronto, then used the memory extraction file to create the rest."

I sat back in my seat. Daniel removed his hand and settled back, too, looking perfectly at ease.

At least the annoyance I'd felt earlier didn't return, and since the three women across from me seemed more interested in the report than glaring at me again, it seemed we had all moved on to bigger things versus petty grievances.

I awkwardly clasped my hands together and leaned closer to Logan, my brow furrowing as I studied his tablet. "What are those tablet things, anyway?"

He angled his body my way, causing a hint of his sandalwood scent to tickle my nose. My lady bits tightened *again*.

"They're normal tablets that the witches have added a few magical qualities to," he explained. "It's how we document everything, communicate, and access database files." Logan swiped across the screen, pulling up another part of Xanthia's brief. A glowing holograph popped up above the screen, hovering in midair.

My eyes bulged when a 3D image of Rigarion snapped his pincers at me.

Wes gestured to Xanthia. "Shall we begin?"

Xanthia stood and paced a few feet before saying, "Our journey to the underworld proved successful. Thanks to Daria and Daniel's help, we were able to learn who's behind the SF attacks—a sorcerer by the name of Stephen Price. He's managed to create a portal to allow low-ranking demons and dragons to enter earth, but as for why he's decided to attack the SF, we still don't know."

Xanthia continued walking to the end of the table then turned. "And as you all know, before our departure for the underworld, I visited the site north of Boise where a recent attack took place. Considering the burn marks, dragon fire was definitely the culprit, and while in the underworld, we visited my dragons. No more were missing, but two had chain marks around their necks, which means Stephen Price was trying to steal them too."

Wes frowned, his mouth tightening. "Your report says you learned about Stephen Price from one high-ranking demon?"

"That's correct." Xanthia touched her nose ring and twirled it a few times. "As some of my fellow half demons are aware, Rigarion is a high-ranking demon in the underworld. Or perhaps *was* is the more accurate term now." She winked at me before launching into a verbal rundown of what the past three earth days had entailed.

The SF members flipped through their 3D replications of the encounters we'd had while Xanthia continued to explain.

When she got to the part about my facing off against Rigarion to learn the key detail that had led to Stephen's identity, Logan's entire body tensed.

The holographic image showed me battling Rigarion before he effectively swallowed me. A few around the table gasped when that happened.

Daniel, however, smiled in my direction, looking quite pleased at my near consumption while Xanthia continued to explain—in gory detail—how I'd destroyed the demon.

"Daria made it out. Obviously." Xanthia snickered when more gasps emitted from around the table when the 3D encounter showed me blowing up Rigarion from the inside out. "But if she hadn't gone to the extremes she did, I'm not sure Rigarion would have revealed who S was."

"Hold on." Chloe held up a hand. "You're telling me this little witch killed a high-ranking demon with her bare hands after he *swallowed* her? You seriously expect us to believe that?"

Xanthia crossed her arms. "She's half witch and half *angel*, remember? She was kind of created to kill demons, so that shouldn't be surprising. Or did you skim that part of the report?"

Chloe and Priscilla both frowned before Priscilla flipped back through her tablet, a brooding expression on her face when her eyes skimmed the page.

Holly laughed. "Are you sure you're not embellishing, Xanthia? Perhaps you made some of this up for theatrics. The SF has never seen anyone destroy a demon like that."

Xanthia's eyes narrowed. "Since you're a witch, you of all people should know these 3D images don't lie since they're from your species' memory extraction magic. Or are you saying witch magic is flawed?"

Holly bristled, tossing her hair over her shoulder, but when she darted a look at me again, some of her cockiness faded, a new wariness taking its place.

"Can we get back to the important information?" Wes held up a hand. "Rigarion identified Stephen Price as the sorcerer who's created a portal that has allowed hell's creatures to permeate earth. Is that what you're saying, Xanthia?"

"That's correct, sir."

Wes stood. "In that case, data and MF squads? Come with me. We need to locate Stephen and discover who's working with him. The rest of you, return to your quarters and get some sleep. Report back to headquarters at oh eight hundred. If we can locate Stephen, we're going after him tomorrow."

Chapter 22

Tomorrow? They're going after Stephen Price tomorrow? My mind reeled at how quickly everything was progressing.

I pushed my chair back as everyone funneled out the door. The three squads that followed Wes continually pushed their glasses up their noses while wearing determined expressions.

"Who are they?" I asked Logan as Daniel, Xanthia, and I followed him, Jake, Brodie, and Alexander out. I didn't look at Holly, Chloe, or Priscilla. Their interest in me seemed to have vanished.

Logan cupped my elbow. "Those are the data and magical forensic specialists. They're the ones behind our international tracking. For the most part, they never leave this building, but we couldn't do our jobs without them since they help locate supes worldwide on the run."

"Like Zach?" I asked, referring to the rogue who'd attacked me and escaped.

His jaw tightened. "Yeah, like Zach. Rogues are some of the supes they try to locate, but rogues are notoriously evasive. Sorcerers, on the other hand, are easier to find."

I remembered Logan's earlier stories about how dangerous their jobs could be. And he could be leaving to battle the very sorcerer that had been killing dozens of SF members.

A sorcerer who had demons and a dragon on his side.

A chill ran through me. I rubbed my hands on my bare forearms as everyone pushed through the exterior doors, heading toward the barracks. The group thinned the farther we went as squad members returned to their apartments.

"This is me," Xanthia said when the third building appeared. "My home away from home."

I surveyed the brick building. "So this is where you live when you're not in California?"

"Yep. When the SF calls, this is where I crash." She hooked a thumb toward the building.

"Are you still going back to the underworld to guard your dragons?"

She shook her head glumly. "I would, but I have a feeling I wouldn't make it out alive if I did, not after the shit we just pulled. As much as I want to stand guard over them, it's just too dangerous right now."

I raised my eyebrows. The fact that Xanthia was still afraid spoke volumes about the unease rippling through the community.

"See you wolves and angels in the morning." She gave everyone a crooked smile.

I managed a nod before Xanthia disappeared into her building.

"Young angel, I shall leave you, too, and return to the *bus*." Daniel's turquoise eyes reflected the moonlight. "In the morning, I shall find you."

"Yeah, okay, that sounds good." I said good night to my angel friend before he tipped his head and disappeared. From there, Logan, Brodie, Jake, Alexander, and I carried on as more from the meeting followed.

With every step we took, and with every SF member that returned to their apartments, the reality of what the next day would bring grew more and more real.

"See you in the morning, bro," Brodie said when he, Alexander, and Jake reached their building.

"Try to get some sleep," Logan replied. "I have a feeling we're all going to need it."

My stomach twisted into knots as the remaining SF members filtered into the building. When it was just Logan and me, our feet tapped on the pavement as we headed toward the very end of the barracks.

The black nighttime sky created a void above us, but dawn would come in just a few hours. Wes had to know that sleep would be impossible, especially with the tension that had oozed from those leaving the meeting.

"Logan?" I stopped midstep, my breath catching. Fresh nighttime scents filled the air around us, but I barely noticed it. I pushed my hair behind my ear, my fingers shaking. "Tomorrow, you could—" Ice filled my belly, chilling me from the inside out. My breath came faster.

He stepped to my side and lifted me into his arms. "I'll be fine," he said, burying his face in my hair.

I clung to him. My fingers twisted around his neck as I relished feeling him, but fear still clawed at my gut. "But Stephen has demons and a dragon."

My powers hummed. Memories of Jayden, Niles, and Zach filled my mind, then came the feeling of being suffocated inside of Rigarion. I trembled, shaking so violently that Logan's grip tightened.

"You don't know what they're like," I whispered. "Demons are strong. So *incredibly* strong, Logan. What if—" I swallowed tightly.

What if he doesn't come back?

He pulled back and cupped my face between his hands, his palms hot against my cool skin. In the dark night, his eyes bored into mine. "I'll come back. I promise."

"But what if you don't?" Tears choked my voice.

His grip tightened. "I will."

But his reassurances didn't alleviate the terror that clenched my throat. In a few short hours, Logan and the squads would be facing unknown odds. It was possible I would never see him again.

What if tonight is the last night we have together?

I pulled him back to me, wanting to touch him, *needing* to touch him and have him stop the aching fear in my chest.

"Touch me. Please. Now," I whispered. "I need you. I need to feel you. I need to know that you're alive and okay."

He didn't question my sudden urgency. He scooped me into his arms and raced the remaining distance to his barrack then to his apartment.

Logan pushed his front door open so violently it sounded as though it broke off the hinges. But any concerns over splintered doorways vanished the second we stepped into his home.

He locked his arms around me, his hands in my hair, his mouth everywhere.

I arched against him, my head falling back as he slammed the door closed behind us, his dark apartment enveloping us. He locked my legs around his waist before striding toward the bedroom, his mouth never breaking contact from mine.

He tasted good. *So* good—better than I remembered.

And his smell was everywhere. I could drown in his scent.

Pale moonlight flooded the floor when he stepped into the master bedroom. The broken furniture and cracked drywall had been repaired from my blasting angel light the other week. Not one crack remained.

We both fell onto the huge mattress.

"Daria," Logan groaned. He moved down my neck, pressing urgent kisses along my skin.

I arched more against him, a moan escaping me. "I want you, Logan. Now!"

The demand left my lips in a throaty whisper. My

core felt on fire—fear and desire turning into one.

Logan sat back, breaking contact between us long enough to strip his shirt off.

My breath hitched. His chest—beautiful, sculpted, and so very powerful—looked even more breathtaking in the moonlight. Every hard dip and angle begged for my touch.

I instinctively sat up, reaching for him. My fingers skimmed along the surface of his stomach. His muscles jumped as he sucked in a breath, his eyes closing and his jaw clenching.

"Daria." He opened his eyes, his irises glowing, and reached for my worn blue shirt. With one deft movement, it was over my head.

My nipples immediately hardened, demanding Logan's touch, needing his mouth.

The glow in his eyes intensified. "Your skin," he murmured.

Since my shirt was off, the subtle glow of my angel powers lit the room like a soft nightlight.

"I don't know how to temper it."

"You're beautiful. I've never seen a woman as beautiful as you." He reached behind me, his lips claiming mine again. His tongue plunged into my mouth as his fingers deftly lifted the bra up and over my head.

The garment fell away, and my boobs spilled out.

His breath sucked in just as his large hands cupped their heavy weight. His thumbs flickered over my nipples, brushing them with the barest contact. I cried out, bucking against him.

"Fuck, your tits are amazing."

He pushed me back on the bed, the movement rough and desperate, then he was on me.

His mouth descended again, taking one large, taut nipple into his velvety smoothness. As soon as his lips closed over my breast, all coherent thought left me.

I still wore the SF pants, and I fumbled with them awkwardly until they were off and kicked to the side. Somehow, Logan's pants disappeared too. All the while, his mouth never left my tits.

My core grew so damned hot with need that my slick folds moistened my thighs when he parted them.

"Fuck, Daria," he whispered. "Fuck, I want you."

"Yes. Now." They were the only words I could manage. Any thoughts of never having sex before, of not knowing what I was doing, vanished. All I could think about was the feel of Logan's hard, throbbing length against my thigh.

I reached down, instinctively wrapping my hand around his velvety steel. His entire body shuddered when I pulled at him, guiding him toward my center.

"Logan. Logan. Please. I need."

"Yes."

Then the tip of his cock was there—right where I wanted it. My entire body quivered. I needed him inside me. I'd never needed anything so badly in my life.

I worked my legs up his back, pushing him, begging him to shift closer to me. He growled and leaned down, his hard chest pressing against my soft breasts while my nipples felt as if they were on fire.

He reached around me and cupped my ass, lifting my hips. The tip of his cock pushed against my heat. Sweat beaded on his lip. I arched more, wanting him so badly that a soft mewling sound escaped me.

"Do you know I've been dreaming about this since the first day I met you?"

I lifted my hips more. "Me too."

His breath hissed in, and then he was sliding into me. Inch by inch.

My body expanded, accommodating his hard length. He stretched and stretched me. His width made me whimper in pain and pleasure. He was so freakin' *huge*.

He paused, seeming to sense my need to adjust to him. "Are you okay?"

But all I could manage was a small nod. I needed him farther. Deeper. I needed him rubbing deeper inside me. "Don't stop."

His jaw clenched more, his expression strained. "I always knew you would feel good, but damn, woman, I've never felt anything so incredible."

He pushed into me again, sliding in slowly, so agonizingly slowly, and my pussy sang with need, but then he slowed.

"Sweet Jesus." He breathed heavily. "I'm sorry, but having me fully in you is probably going to hurt."

"Don't stop!" I wiggled more, and another breath hissed out of him.

And with one final thrust, he buried his length inside me.

I screamed at the onslaught. Pain and pleasure ripped

through me. I wanted him inside me, *needed* it, but at the same time it hurt like a bitch.

"I'm sorry, babe." He kissed the side of my neck, his heavy weight pressing down on me. "You're a virgin, and I've been told with virgins it usually hurts the first time." A growl rumbled from his throat, a very contented grumble. "You've never had anyone else's dick inside you. Just mine." His liquid-gold irises gleamed with satisfaction.

"I only ever want you inside me."

Another contented growl came from him before he moved, pulling out a few inches.

I gasped, some of the pressure releasing, but that empty feeling returned. I wiggled again as the pain lessened. "Come back."

He smiled, his firm lips tilting up. "I'm not going anywhere." He pushed forward again, his hard length filling me.

A moan tore from my lips. *Hot damn.* He felt so incredibly good.

"You like that?"

But I couldn't reply. My senses again became consumed with Logan—his scent, his cock, the feel of his entire body's weight pressed against mine. I pushed up with my hips, wanting him sheathed completely in me.

He sucked in another breath then began moving in earnest. Time lost all meaning as Logan pumped into me again and again.

My body turned to fire. My nerves electrified.

I met each demanding thrust with a rise of my hips,

instinct taking over as I raked my fingers up and down his back while moaning in pleasure at the exquisite feelings he evoked in my core.

Pressure built inside me, growing higher and higher with every thrust, every flick of my nipple, every kiss and demanding push from the werewolf who dominated my body.

"That's it, babe." He thrust more, each plunge going deeper and harder as he inhaled my scent again and again. "Fuck, you're aroused, Dar. I can't get enough of it."

"Logan . . ." I writhed against him, needing to reach the edge, but it kept growing higher. "Logan . . ."

He pushed up more on his elbow, his hips slamming against my core again and again, the movement growing faster and harder.

I gripped his buttocks, the hard globes slick with sweat as he rammed into me.

"Yes. More. Don't stop!"

He increased his rhythm, groaning as he penetrated me relentlessly.

The feel of him filling me, dominating me, and fucking me like I'd never been fucked before made a tidal wave rise higher and higher, building toward a mountainous tip.

"Yes, Dar. I can smell that you're about to cum." He growled and slammed into me again. "Cum for me, babe. Cum hard."

I screamed when an orgasm rocked my core, making me buck wildly.

Logan groaned and grasped my hips, his fingers

digging into my soft flesh as he roared his release, his cock pumping, his seed shooting from his body so powerfully that I felt the hot wetness filling me.

I kept screaming, my entire body trembling. My orgasm went on and on, the never-ending waves pounding into me again and again as Logan's cock filled me completely.

He held me close, his grip never lessening as my virginal body became a thing of the past.

"Damn, babe," he finally whispered when the trembles subsided. "You're fucking incredible."

When the last of his seed released, he collapsed on top of me and rolled onto his side, pulling me with him, our bodies still joined. I panted quietly and rested my head on his arm. Behind him, the hint of the sun peeked through the curtains.

I trembled again, my angel powers continuing to flow. During sex, I hadn't noticed them, but they hummed within me again, languidly rolling around, their power right there, waiting to be tapped.

For a moment, I couldn't breathe, only feel.

Sweat coated my body. Logan's scent permeated my skin. My angels powers hummed, in tune with my existence.

In one word, everything was *perfect*.

A smile grew on my lips as the enormity of what I'd just done settled in. I wasn't a virgin anymore. I'd not only had sex, but I'd had mind-blowing, rock-my-world, holy-fucking-cow kind of sex.

I had no idea my body was capable of feeling that

way.

"You look happy." Logan propped himself up on an elbow, smiling lazily.

"I am."

A tender look crossed his face, then he lifted a finger, tracing it across my cheek. "What have you done to me, Daria Gresham?" He pushed the damp hair from my face as his cock grew soft inside me.

I relished the feel of it. I relished every moment of it.

"Nothing you haven't done to me," I whispered.

"I'm never letting you go. You know that, right?"

My lips parted, but I couldn't speak, not after the enormity of what he'd just.

After a moment, I finally managed to reply, "But what about Crystal? What about me not being a werewolf?"

I hated uttering her name in his bed, after something sacred had passed between us, but the thought of her, of what waited back home for him, always lingered in the back of my mind.

Always.

Like a buzzing fly that wouldn't leave me in peace.

For the merest second, Logan's jaw tightened, then he forced a smile. "We'll figure it out. I'm not letting you go, and I won't let them take you from me." An edge filled his tone, hinting at the alpha power within him.

Shivering, I wrapped my arms around him. I could only hope that he was right.

∞ ∞ ∞

The faint grayness of dawn eventually gave way to hazy red as Logan made love to me again and again. A part of me knew we were both trying to forget the inevitable.

Neither of us wanted to face it.

But whether or not either of us wanted to admit it, outside of Logan's small apartment, with its modern décor and firm king-sized bed—reality waited.

Logan was an alpha with a pack that expected him to lead.

A fiancée waited for him back home, and if he didn't marry her, a werewolf war would begin.

I was a half-angel, half-witch who still had a list of sick clients waiting for her return.

And somewhere out there, Stephen Price waited. If the sorcerer had been located, Logan would be leaving in a few short hours, and I didn't know if he would come back.

But at that moment, none of it mattered.

Logan and I were together, as we'd both wanted to be from the moment we'd laid eyes on one another, and nothing could come between us.

Logan's insatiable appetite only seemed to grow with every joining we shared. Just when I thought for sure that we would doze off for a few minutes of sleep, he would pull me into his arms, his cock hardening against my thigh, then the stirrings of desire would swirl in my belly, despite the fact that he'd just given me a mind-blowing orgasm not even fifteen minutes prior.

It was all so perfect. I didn't want it to end.

But time had a different agenda. Eventually, the sun

rose in earnest, and a new day began.

My legs felt like jelly when I finally slid out of Logan's bed, his arm tightening around me before letting me go.

"Where are you going?" he asked, his voice husky.

"To the bathroom. I'll be right back." A moment of modesty made my cheeks heat as I sauntered bare-assed out of the room, but a low growl hummed in Logan's throat. I was beginning to learn that meant he wanted more. My flush turned into a smile.

In the bathroom, I brushed my teeth and cleaned the tender skin between my thighs. Logan's seed had spilled into me again and again, before it all slipped out, making my thighs sticky.

I relished the foreign feel, though, but it was only when I was washing it away that reality penetrated the thin veil of intimacy that we'd woven around us.

Logan and I had just had unprotected sex.

A *lot* of unprotected sex.

And while diseases weren't something I worried about as a supernatural, pregnancy was something else entirely.

I slapped a hand to my forehead, in complete disbelief at how irresponsible we'd both been. "Real, freakin' mature, Dar. Mom would be so proud," I whispered.

If Cecile knew what I had just done, she would pull her hair out. It was Cecile who'd thoroughly educated me on the birds and the bees. Mom and Nan had been more caught up in potential mates and explaining how our magic worked to divulge too many details on human anatomy, but Cecile had been another story. She'd made sure I knew all about a woman's womb.

I quickly counted back the days from my last period and breathed a sigh of relief that my period was due any day. The chances of me getting pregnant were small. Of course, nothing was a guarantee, but conception was unlikely.

Still, we'd been irresponsible.

We couldn't keep doing that.

Shaking my head, I was about to pad back to the room when Logan knocked softly on the door. A smile curved my lips when his sandalwood scent, tinged with musky sex, washed into the small room as he peeked through the crack in the door.

"Did you get lost in here?"

My smile grew. "I was just coming back. I wanted—"

BOOM!

A loud explosion rocked the building, nearly knocking me over as drywall dust shook from the walls.

"What the hell?" I whispered, my heart slamming against my ribs as I gripped the sink's edge.

The door swung violently open. Logan stood in the doorway, his bare chest still glistening with sweat, but boxers covered his lower half.

"Dar? Are you okay?" He rushed to my side.

"Yeah, I'm fine, but what the hell was—"

BOOM!

A second explosion rocked the building, the walls shuddering violently. Logan wrapped his arms around me, protecting me from falling debris. His whipped his head up, his nostrils flaring.

A dark glow lit his eyes. "We're under attack."

The second the words left his mouth, a siren wailed.

"Shit!" He scooped me into his arms and, in a blurred move, transported us to his bedroom.

Through the windows, I could see SF vehicles mobilizing around headquarters, but what I saw in the sky made my lips part with horror.

"Logan! Look!"

He grabbed the clothes he was pulling from his drawer and was at my side in less than a second.

"He's here." The statement came out in a low whisper as I wrapped my arms around myself.

In the sky, an army of supernaturals rode dragons. They headed right for headquarters as the sorcerer leading them threw explosive spells at the buildings one by one.

Stephen Price had arrived, and nobody had known that he was coming.

Chapter 23

"We need to get out of here. Now!" Logan whipped me away from the window just as one of the dragons opened its mouth and spewed fire at an SF building.

The concrete erupted into flames, the manmade stone no match for dragon fire.

Another explosion rocked the grounds when Stephen threw a magical bomb. The flaming blue sphere blasted through a bunker on the opposite side of the base.

"What do we do?" I scrambled into my clothes from the previous night as the walls shook violently again when another magical bomb went off across the courtyard.

"You need to get into the underground bunker. Now. You'll be safe there." He grabbed my arm and pulled me from the room just as the window exploded behind us.

Shards of glass flew everywhere, but Logan already had me positioned in front of him, his large frame taking the brunt of the blow.

"But what about you?" I screeched as another explosion made the ground tremble violently.

"I'll be fine. I just need to get you safe."

We were out the front door and in the hallway before I could take another breath. Logan ran, keeping my hand tightly in his grasp. We collided with other supernaturals who were also fleeing.

My angel powers hummed, growing stronger as the demons advanced.

Evil was coming.

I could feel it.

I tried to round the corner to the main exterior door, but Logan pulled me down another hallway. "Not that way. This way."

Another blast shook the walls, the building groaning as SF members scrambled from their apartments. Everyone hurried into the halls like ants escaping an anthill.

I struggled to keep up with Logan's long strides, my hair flying in wild tendrils around my face. The outdoor siren continued to blare, its wail making my heart pound even faster.

"What about Cecile and Mike?" I asked as everyone ran down a back stairwell in single file.

"I don't know. I can only hope the sorcerers' barrier will keep them safe."

"So you think humans have no idea that dragons are

flying in the sky?"

"I don't know. Possibly, but right now, I'm not concerned about that. We need to move. I need to get you safe." His grip on me tightened as we flew down the steps.

Around us SF members moved quickly. Seeing the hurried yet calm and coordinated way in which everyone acted made me realize I was the lone woman freaking out.

They were all trained SF members and knew exactly what to do and where to go if headquarters were attacked.

But then I caught the wild-eyed look of a fairy with straight purple hair, and the clenching fists of a man who was probably a werewolf given his frame. Everyone might be trained, but a battle had just been sprung upon everyone without warning. Fear shone in their eyes.

Logan increased his pace, taking the stairs down two at a time. When I struggled to keep up, he scooped me into his arms and carried me in a jostling run until we burst through the bottom door.

A large tunnel stretched out in front of us, overhead lights illuminating the space. Doors dotted the hallway as far as I could see. All of them were open as SF members poured into the escape route.

"What is this place?" I anxiously looked around for Logan's squad and Xanthia. So far, I hadn't seen anybody I recognized.

"They're tunnels that funnel to the main headquarter building. They're for emergency use only." Logan sidestepped a man who was hobbling, blood trailing down his leg. He must have been injured in one of the explosions.

"We need to help him." I gripped Logan's shoulders tightly. My powers hummed, my healing instincts kicking into action.

Logan shook his head. "Protocol dictates that everybody mobilize immediately to headquarters. He's in the tunnels. He'll be safe. But we can't be clogging the route by stopping to tend to the wounded right now."

I clamped my jaw shut, feeling entirely out of my depth. Even though I'd helped the SF with their mission in the underworld, in reality, I knew nothing about how the elite group worked.

"Daria!" Xanthia waved frantically behind us.

"Xanthia! Logan, stop! Xanthia just came out of one of the doors." Perched above Logan's shoulder, I had a superior view of the tunnel. "And there's Brodie, Jake, and Alexander!"

Logan's squad hurried to reach us, Xanthia hot on their tail.

"We're seriously under attack?" Brodie's blue eyes appeared electric when he reached us.

Logan hadn't slowed, despite my plea, but his pack brothers fell into a run beside him. It was the first time I'd seen Alexander without his glasses.

Even though they all sprinted, Xanthia still kept up, but her bright-red cheeks showed that she couldn't for long. No half demon had the conditioning of a werewolf.

"Logan, slow down!" I struggled in his grip. The hard bumps from the run jarred my rib cage.

"We're almost there."

Struggling more, I said, "I mean it, Logan. Xanthia's falling behind. You need to let me go!"

He slowed his pace then stopped as dozens of SF members filed past us.

I slipped from his arms and ran to Xanthia. A tall woman with wicked-looking fairy teeth, knocked into me on her jog past.

Trying to stay out of everyone's way, I pulled Xanthia to the wall.

"They have dragons." I panted from the adrenaline. "Did you see them?"

Xanthia gave a curt nod and placed her hands on her hips, her chest heaving. "I saw. I counted at least a hundred demon-possessed on each of their backs. They have Drakon, Roofessee, and Quaneely. They must have stolen Drakon and Roofessee right after we left, probably being alerted that we were on to them." She seethed more. "They're all babies, less than a year old. Don't let their size fool you, cause they're all Magnus Dragarions, the largest breed, but they're untrained. They're flying in fear right now. I could see it in their flames."

"Their flames?"

"Their flames are longer than normal, probably hotter too. That means they're shooting fire because they're afraid. That bastard is terrorizing them."

"Daria!" Logan yelled.

I took Xanthia's hand and pulled her toward him. When her hot fingers slid into mine, it again struck me that I could touch people.

You're stronger than you think, young angel.

Daniel's words came back to me, reminding me of how far I'd come.

"We need to get you to the bunker," Logan said when we reached him. He grabbed my wrist, but I straightened and pulled away, my resolve strengthening.

"No, I'm not hiding. I know I'm not a trained SF member, but I *am* part angel." I held up my arm. The glow of my angel powers had intensified as a war raged above us.

I could *feel* the demons.

My dark and light powers buzzed, growing stronger with every passing second. The sheer strength of my angelic lineage hummed through my veins, that raw unspent energy electrifying my nerves, the feeling reminding me that I *was* strong.

I was capable.

And I was born to do this.

"I can fight them, Logan. I can kill them with my bare hands."

The color drained from Logan's face. "Daria, no. You're not fighting."

He gripped my arm harder, and my powers flared. I let them rise up, just a fraction until he felt their strength.

"Shit!" His hand flew off me as red light puffed from my skin. "What the hell?"

I stepped closer to him as I pulled my powers back inside. "Please, Logan. Trust me. I'm not helpless anymore. Whether or not you want to admit it, what's going on up there"—I pointed toward the ceiling as another tremble shook the earth—"is what I was meant to banish. My father was an archangel. His blood flows through my veins. My purpose is not just to heal. It's also to banish evil, and right now . . . evil is upon us."

Chapter 24

Logan's jaw clenched tighter, and that groove appeared between his eyes.

"Trust me," I whispered.

"Um . . . guys, we need to go." Brodie shuffled beside us. Already, the SF members in the tunnel had thinned. Most had already reached the main building.

Logan nodded stiffly, and once again, we all took off.

"I don't know if I can watch you out there," Logan said through clenched teeth. The wolves had slowed their run so Xanthia and I could keep up, but I still breathed heavily.

"Then don't watch me. Concentrate on you. It's probably better that way. I'll just distract you."

Brodie grinned at me. "I, for one, can't wait to see

you in action, Dar. You really killed a high-ranking demon on your own?"

"She did indeed," came a musical voice.

I shrieked when Daniel materialized beside us. He appeared out of thin air, running with us and keeping pace as if we were out for an afternoon stroll.

My heart pounded harder, making my blood rush.

"You scared the crap out of me." I nudged him and sucked in another lungful of air. "But I'm glad you're here. Did you see what's going on up there?"

"Oh, yes. I felt them coming. I would have come sooner, but I wanted to ensure that Cecile and Mike were safely removed from the area so no harm would come to them or the *bus*."

I breathed a sigh of relief just as the doors to headquarters appeared. "Thank you."

"My pleasure, young angel."

We all raced into the main building. I followed Logan and his squad into a cavernous, domed space.

Inside the circular room, every SF member was donning military garb and helmets, brandishing weapons, and activating glowing devices on their wrists. From there, they ran into a circular tube in the center of the room before shooting upward and disappearing above.

"What do I do?" I asked.

"Civilians are supposed to report to the bunker." Logan stood at my side, a wild look in his eyes.

Jake, Alexander, and Brodie all clamped glowing devices around their wrists before stripping their clothes and dropping to the floor.

Hair sprouted on their arms, their faces elongated, and within seconds, they shimmered between the image of wolf and man. Another second passed, and three huge wolves stood at our sides, the glowing devices encircling their front legs.

"I'm not hiding," I replied.

His jaw locked again, but he nodded curtly. "Fine, but please, Dar, don't do anything stupid. If you think you're in danger, and if you don't think you can stay safe, please retreat."

"I will."

"Daria shall be fine, Logan. You have nothing to fear." Daniel's calm words were the only serene sounds in the chaotic room.

Some of the tightness around Logan's mouth abated. "There's no time for me to get approval from Wes for both of you to join us." He ripped his shirt off before slapping a glowing device around his wrist. His bare muscles looked tanned and hard. "But we'll have to deal with any fallout later."

He pulled me into his arms and kissed me hard. His warm, sweet breath puffed against my ear when he pulled back and whispered, "I'd rather die than see you hurt. Please stay safe."

I held him tightly, one final hug before replying, "I will. I promise."

He let go, and Brodie whined anxiously. But in a blink and shimmer of magic, Logan shifted. He could shift faster than any werewolf I'd seen.

Logan gave me one final look, a soft whine erupting

from his mouth, before the four of them loped to the circular chamber and disappeared into the war above.

"You want a weapon?" Xanthia asked. She grabbed a wicked-looking gun before throwing on a crisscross chest harness with metal stars attached. "My lasso is no good out of hell, but these . . ." She tossed a jagged piece of metal. "Throwing stars are my favorite, and this comes in handy too." She lifted the gun. Purple light illuminated one of the chambers. "One shot from this penetrates a sorcerer's barrier spell."

Considering I had no idea how to use any of the SF's weapons—or any weapon for that matter—I shook my head then held up my hands. "I think these are my best option."

Xanthia snickered. "That's so badass." She holstered the gun and grabbed my hand before calling, "Come on, Daniel. We don't want to miss all the fun."

She grinned, that crazy gleam in her eyes again. The demon within her shone strongly, and I once again felt thankful she was only a half demon whose soul was more good than bad.

My powers zapped when the three of us dove into the room's center chamber. I could feel the full-blooded demons since they were so close, but unlike Daniel, I hadn't felt them coming.

A burst of air rushed around us as we accelerated upward in the vacuum. I shrieked, more from surprise than the speed, but Xanthia just laughed and let out a whoop.

We emerged above ground, the magical evacuation

chamber disappearing. Solid ground materialized beneath our feet.

Around us, chaos reigned.

In other areas above ground, more SF members popped up from the subterranean chambers, making me realize the magical vacuum chamber we'd emerged from had more than one exit.

Xanthia grabbed my hand and ducked just as a stream of blue flashed over us. Red-eyed supernaturals prowled the grounds, the dragons having dropped them off.

"Get to as many of the demon-possessed as you can." She ripped a star from her chest. "If I can get to my dragons, I should be able to command them, but getting to them is going to be the hard part. Daniel, I could use your help with that."

Daniel crouched beside us, and his shirt ripped away. "I'm happy to oblige."

His thick, feathery wings sprouted from his back, but his gaze stayed on Stephen, who flew in the sky, leading two other supernaturals astride the dragons.

Around us, red-eyed supernaturals battled with SF members. Screams, gunfire, magical blasts, and roars from the dragons filled the air.

Only twenty feet away, a red-eyed vampire wrestled with a werewolf. The wolf snarled, biting one of the vampire's arms before ripping it from his body.

The vampire hissed but kept fighting as blood spewed from his arm socket. Then the gushing abruptly stopped, and the limb began to regenerate.

On the other side of us, a witch and a sorcerer

squared off, blasting each other at crazy intervals, diving at the last moment to avoid the other's spells. They seemed evenly matched.

My breath came faster as I began to doubt myself.

I was a healer.

I wasn't a fighter.

Logan was right. How could I do this?

As if sensing my distress, Daniel placed his hand on mine.

"Get ready, Daniel." Xanthia grinned. "I'm going to have a little fun first, but then I'll need your help." She flew from our side, a wild banshee scream tearing from her mouth as she whizzed away.

She threw her stars in quick succession, hitting every red-eyed possessed supernatural in her path.

One star hit the vampire who was battling the werewolf. It embedded itself right where his heart lay, causing him to explode into ash, the gray powdery substance coating the wolf.

The werewolf shook himself clean before taking a giant leap to pounce on a red-eyed fairy over fifteen feet away.

With a rip from his powerful jaws, the wolf beheaded the fairy, and her body fell to the ground.

My breath came even faster, my heart pounding more. It thumped so hard that it felt as if it would beat right out of my chest.

"Remember who you are, young angel." Daniel's calm words broke through the horrific feeling that threatened to suffocate me. "Remember whose blood swirls through your veins."

I squeezed his hand tightly. His words evoked memories of my mother and my nan. They'd too said something similar whenever I doubted myself.

"I'm a Gresham," I whispered to myself.

More than ever, I knew what that meant.

I was half archangel, half witch, possibly the only being walking the earth who possessed that rare lineage.

My angel powers hummed and swirled, rising to the surface as I called them forth. A deep sense of calmness and purpose settled within me.

I squeezed Daniel's hand one last time. "I'll be fine."

With a satisfied nod, he let go of me and launched himself into the air. He flew upward, ducking or spiraling anytime a demon-possessed sorcerer tried to blast him from above or below. I knew where he was heading—the dragons.

They were Stephen's best weapons, wreaking havoc on the earth, incinerating buildings and SF members in their paths.

Daniel knocked a red-eyed supernatural from one of the dragons before swooping back to the ground to grab Xanthia.

I could have sworn I heard her excited whoop as his arms encircled her and he launched high into the sky, dodging the blasts and spells as one of the giant dragons roared, no longer being commanded by a rider.

But I didn't have time to see if she and Daniel made it to the dragon. Two red-eyed supernaturals ran toward me. I readied myself, my powers strengthening. One, a female vampire, hissed and reached for my neck.

I dodged just in time and grabbed her hand, letting my angel powers burst forth.

She imploded the moment I let my powers rush into her. A surprised look filled her face in the second before she died.

The other supernatural jumped back, on the balls of his feet. He stood at least six-six, and I guessed he was a rogue who hadn't shifted. Either that, or a sorcerer.

When he held his palm up, blue swirled into a ball, meaning my second guess was right.

I sank to the ground and rolled out of the way just as the ball released from his hand and rocketed into the ground where I'd crouched only moments before.

I sprang onto his back, and my powers buzzed out of me.

He didn't have time to react before my angel powers obliterated him.

Dodging, running, and grabbing every demon-possessed I could find, I worked as quickly as I could. The other SF members soon caught on to what I was capable of.

Some shouted my name, holding thrashing demon-possessed supernaturals in place for me to annihilate.

I would run to them, grab the possessed, and let my powers banish the demon that dared to ravage earth.

My angel powers grew stronger, my movements more sure as I ran and dodged spells. Sweat trailed down my back and along my ear as I touched and killed every demon I could find.

"No!" The scream penetrated the blasting sounds of weapons and spells.

I darted my gaze around, searching for the source.

Only fifteen yards away, two demon-possessed rogues in wolf form held an SF member down. A third clamped onto her leg, biting deeply into her flesh.

My heart pounded harder, horrifying memories of Jayden, Niles, and Zach doing something very similar to me coming to my mind.

The woman screamed again, pain making her yells shrill. Despite her kicking the werewolf with her free foot, the rogue wouldn't dislodge.

Ignoring my fear, I sprinted toward her, jumped onto the rogue's back, and encircled my hands around his furry neck. Then a blast of red light shot from my palms.

A high-pitched yelp followed before the rogue turned into gelatinous goo, his entire body pulverized from my power.

The other two rogues that held the woman eyed me warily. One let go of the woman's arm and lunged.

I caught his throat when he was in midair. He imploded the second I touched him.

The third rogue dropped the woman's arm and attempted to flee.

"No, you don't!" She clamped her hand around his leg. It slowed him down enough for me to grip his furry tail.

Despite the minimal contact, my angel powers still shot into him. A panicked yelp was the last sound he made before he turned to mush.

I collapsed to the ground, breathing heavily.

"Are you okay?" My eyes widened when I saw who lay on the ground. "Chloe?"

The fairy's spiky red hair was covered by a helmet, but her goggles had dislodged, and her startling green eyes met mine. For a moment, she actually looked embarrassed. "Yeah, it's me. Thanks."

I helped her up, and despite limping, she stayed upright.

I eyed her leg. "Are you going to be able to—"

She shoved me aside as a blue blast hit the concrete building behind us. "Get down!" She pulled up her weapon and aimed.

One shot from her gun, and the sorcerer who'd tried to kill us fell.

She swiveled her gun around. "I've got you covered. Move!"

I didn't question her order. I sprinted toward the fighting, searching for my next demon victim.

At the end of the base, near the remaining freestanding barracks, I snaked my fingers around a fairy's ankle.

She bared her teeth, but a blast of my powers had her head tipping back in a scream before she exploded.

I moved quickly again, darting from demon to demon to work my power.

When the area cleared, the SF members who were still alive ran off.

My stomach twisted as I looked around at the dead. Bloody bodies littered the ground.

I still hadn't seen Logan.

I had no idea where he fought, and since I hadn't seen Wes either, I guessed that the SF general was stationed somewhere, calling the shots and telling the squads what to do.

Not too far away, one of the wrist bands crackled on a fallen SF member. I knew those devices were how they communicated with each other. Perhaps I could detach one from the dead and contact Logan.

I kept my back pressed against a building, anxiously looking for where the fighting was. The last thing I needed was a demon catching me unawares as I crouched over a dead SF member.

Smoke filled the air. Shielding my eyes, I surveyed the hazy sky. Stephen still rode his dragon, but my shoulders sagged with relief when I spotted Daniel still flying and Xanthia riding another dragon.

Together, they were working tirelessly to dislodge Stephen, but every time they got close, he would send out a horrific blast.

SF members on the ground were firing, too, but it appeared that no SF weapon could penetrate the magical spell surrounding Stephen. Like a force field, it deflected all of the weapons' blasts, despite Xanthia claiming her glowing purple gun could penetrate a sorcerer's spell.

"Damn him!" I seethed quietly.

I took some pleasure in seeing that Xanthia now commanded Roofessee and Drakon. She rode one, the other flying at her side. The free-flying dragon continually cocked its head toward Xanthia, as if asking what to do next. At a flick of her hand or a yell from her mouth, the young dragon would respond, swooshing or diving around Stephen.

But Stephen still commanded Quaneely relentlessly. The female dragon screamed continuously under the sorcerer's cruel control.

Breathing heavily, I watched them for a moment. More fighting sounded from the opposite end of the base. Adrenaline still pumped through me, but my muscles also quivered. Despite doing my best to stay in shape, I wasn't conditioned for fighting.

Xanthia's dragon abruptly took a terrifying dive and flew right in front of the fire that spewed from Stephen's dragon's mouth.

Jaw dropping, I realized what Xanthia was doing.

She and her dragon were using their bodies to stop the buildings from being incinerated. Xanthia was single-handedly managing to deflect most of Quaneely's fire, flying in front of the flames when necessary to keep them from incinerating more buildings or killing more SF members on the ground.

Her magical demon-mojo-possessed clothing stayed intact, and considering she continued to whoop from the sky, I knew my friend was enjoying her dances with death.

A flash of red eyes caught my attention, bringing my focus back to the ground. My powers instinctively prickled when I spotted two possessed supernaturals stealthily stalking around a destroyed building.

I crept their way, doing my best to keep my footsteps

light.

Ash from dead vampires and goo from dead rogues and demons littered the ground. Several dead SF members also lay still, their vacant eyes staring at the sky.

Bile rose in my throat at the sight of so much death and carnage, but I picked up my pace when the two possessed supernaturals darted around a burning pile of concrete.

I inched around the pile, readying myself to fight.

But nothing greeted me but more ashy earth.

Quaneely screamed again. It appeared Stephen's tactics had abruptly changed. The sorcerer's attention was no longer focused on the ground but instead on his opponents in the sky.

My eyes bulged when he threw his blasting magic toward Xanthia. At the rate it flew, she wouldn't have time to maneuver away.

It was on the tip of my tongue to scream a warning to her when something large and heavy shoved my back.

I shrieked and fell, my jaw cracking on a piece of broken concrete.

Blood rushed into my mouth. I tried to spit it out, but a massive weight pinned me to the ground, squeezing my air out.

Hot saliva dripped into my ear. A deep growl came next.

I tried to scream, and I struggled to reach behind me and make contact with the rogue on my back, but the werewolf opened its mouth over my neck.

Shit!

I tried to heave him off me, my movements turning frantic as his teeth grazed my skin. Pain prickled my neck, but then the rogue yelped, and his weight disappeared.

I flipped around and saw something barrel past me, like a spiral of muscle and fur.

My jaw dropped. An SF werewolf had attacked the rogue.

The SF werewolf and rogue tumbled on the ground, ash and debris coating their fur as they viciously fought.

Flashing teeth, bloodcurdling snarls, and deep growls followed. Everything happened at once. They moved so fast that I had a hard time deciphering who was who.

Then their movements suddenly stopped.

Logan!

In his black wolf form, he had pinned the rogue beneath him, his jaw on his throat. My eyes bulged when I saw who he held.

Zach.

I scrambled to my feet, intent on helping Logan, but he plunged his teeth into Zach's neck. With a wrenching yank, he tore the rogue's throat out.

I skidded to a stop a few yards away.

Logan lifted his head. Blood covered his muzzle, and concrete dust coated his fur, but he still stood strong and appeared uninjured.

He spat the remains of Zach's furry scruff from his mouth and loped to my side, looking me over, as if assessing if I was okay.

"I'm fine," I whispered even though the cut in my mouth still trickled blood. I ran my hands through his black fur and closed my eyes, calling on my angel powers to heal me. Not even a second passed before my cut had sewn shut.

I opened my eyes again and reveled in being so close to Logan. It felt so good to feel him, to know that he was okay. He leaned against me, encircling me and assessing our surroundings, never once letting his guard down.

Logan lifted his head and howled.

Brodie, Alexander, and Jake appeared through a thick cloud of smoke. A horrific crash sounded, and the earth rumbled again. Another SF building had fallen. Stephen's dragon was still wreaking havoc.

"How the hell do we stop him?" I wiped the sweat from my face as Logan and his pack brothers brushed against my sides.

Blood covered all of them, but they still moved well, although Alexander's leg appeared hurt. He limped slightly, but he didn't let it slow him down.

"We need to get him off that drag—"

My voice cut off as heat scorched the land in front of us. A terrifying rush of air grazed my cheeks. My eyes widened with horror.

Stephen and his dragon appeared above us, hovering over the ground.

My jaw dropped when I saw Stephen Price up close.

It's him!

The man who'd been watching me train with Daniel and had later followed me to the café in the supernatural marketplace sat on the huge dragon in front of me.

Logan shoved into me, forcing me to move as his

pack brothers scrambled, but I knew it was no use. The dragon was too close, Xanthia nowhere to be seen.

My stomach sank at what that undoubtedly implied.

It was the only thought that registered in my mind when Stephen raised his arm and Quaneely opened her mouth.

A ball of fire spewed from the dragon, aimed directly at me—the angel Stephen Price knew he needed to kill.

Chapter 25

Logan's jaws clamped around my arm, and he threw me so fast that the entire world turned into a blur.

I hit the ground hard, only to see Quaneely's fire now aiming at Logan.

Panic and despair burst through my body, flooding my senses.

"No!"

I pushed up from the ground, but I wasn't moving fast enough. Fire rolled in Quaneely's mouth, balling on her tongue, like everything was happening in slow motion.

I tripped as I tried to run.

No! Not Logan! Please! Not Logan!

I ran faster, but it wasn't enough.

The fire rolled, the ball turning into a blast.

No!

A ripping sensation tore through my back, and a rush of air followed.

The earth flew past me at a dizzying speed as my feet left the ground.

I slammed into the dragon's neck with everything I had, my angel powers rushing through me and blasting her massive head to the left.

Quaneely gave an ear-piercing roar when my dark power penetrated her skin. Fire shot from her mouth but missed Logan at the last possible second.

It was only when she swung her head back to me, her neck's scales rough and pebbled beneath my hands, that I realized Stephen watched me with surprised-filled eyes. He sat on her back only feet away.

"We meet again, *angel*." His gaze narrowed.

My jaw dropped when I saw the twenty feet of air between my feet and the ground. Giant wings brushed the air behind me, holding me aloft.

My heart beat so hard I couldn't breathe. I'd grown wings.

I'd grown freakin' *wings!*

But I didn't have a chance to adjust to my wings' foreign sensation. Stephen lifted his hand. Blue magic rolled from his palm just as he commanded Quaneely to fly back into the sky.

I struggled to get away from his imminent blast by darting to the side, but my new angel wings clipped the dragon, making me falter.

I began to fall.

Not understanding how my wings had worked before, I frantically reached for something to hold onto as air rushed around me.

Stephen unleashed his blast as Quaneely rose into the sky. A bright blue ball hurtled at me.

I squeezed my eyes tightly closed and screamed when a powerful force barreled into me.

I expected pain to follow or my dark power to rush up and try to save me from Stephen's lethal blow, but neither happened.

When I opened my eyes, strong, muscled arms encircled me as the ground beneath me disappeared.

"I see you've grown wings, young angel." Daniel smiled as he flew us upward. "Now you just need to use them."

The earth disappeared beneath us at a dizzying rate.

I shook my head frantically, my hands clenching his forearms so tightly my knuckles turned white. "What just happened? Did I just really grow wings?"

"Yes. I'm not sure how, but you did."

Above us, Stephen and his dragon flew upward. The dragon's huge wings flapped, lifting them higher and higher.

"Where's Xanthia?" I asked with a panicked voice.

"There." Daniel pointed toward the mountains.

I almost cried in relief when I saw her still astride the first dragon, although she was far away. "Where's the other dragon?"

"Injured. She helped him to one of the

mountaintops."

"That's why she disappeared. I thought—" My breath sucked in as a tidal wave of relief poured through me.

She wasn't dead.

It was crazy how quickly Xanthia had come to mean something to me.

"She's safe, young angel, and it may not feel like it, but we're winning this war. With you taking out so many demons on the ground and Xanthia and I fighting Stephen in the sky, this battle is almost won."

"But not yet," I said. "Look!"

Stephen and Quaneely had switched directions and were flying straight for us, gaining speed.

I clung to Daniel. "He'll be here any minute."

"Fly, young angel. Spread your wings."

"How?"

"Feel them. They're no different from moving your arms. They're a part of you."

I clung to him tighter. "But what if I can't? I'll fall and die."

"You won't. Your wings are like additional limbs. Spread them. Use them as our maker intended."

I closed my eyes and concentrated on my wings. Similar to wanting to lift my arms, I pictured my wings spreading.

Daniel moved aside as my wings unfolded. "That's it. Now, fly." He launched me from his arms.

My stomach dropped, and I waited for that feeling of plunging to the earth, but I continued to imagine my wings keeping me aloft.

When I opened my eyes, I hovered in the air, Daniel at my side.

He grinned.

Air whooshed by my cheeks. I ducked, my wings automatically correcting my position in the sky. Xanthia barreled past us on her dragon, grinning when she spotted me.

"Holy shit, Dar! You've got wings!" She whooped, but her glee didn't last long.

Stephen flew through the clouds like a missile intent on killing us.

Xanthia squared her dragon to face his. He wrenched Quaneely's head back, forcing her to shoot fire at her trainer just as he wielded an explosive spell.

Xanthia dodged, avoiding both. The blue ball hurtled past her.

"We have to penetrate his barrier," Daniel said, staying aloft beside me. "If we don't, he will continue wreaking havoc."

My thoughts raced as Stephen threw another explosive spell at Xanthia. She and her dragon, I didn't know if it was Roofessee or Drakon, hovered in front of us, taking the brunt of Stephen's hits.

"What if we don't go after him, but we . . ." I licked my lips. I knew Xanthia wouldn't like my plan, and I didn't either, but we had to stop Stephen. "What if we go after Quaneely? Without her, Stephen won't be able to fly. He'll possibly die from the fall, and even if he doesn't, on the ground, he won't be as strong."

Daniel nodded. "I tried that, but anytime I got too

close, Quaneely shot fire at me."

"But now there are two of us."

A look of understanding came over his face as atmospheric wind flowed around us. "And if we both come at her at the same time . . ."

"Exactly."

We took off, flying in opposite directions around Stephen. The sorcerer's head shot up, his gaze narrowing when he saw us, but his attention was still focused on Xanthia.

Xanthia dodged another spell, but she moved sluggishly, her biceps straining as she held onto her dragon tightly.

Stephen launched another blue ball as she struggled to shift herself back upright. I opened my mouth to shout a warning, when Stephen swiveled his torso around and blasted a fiery blue ball at me. It hurtled at an alarming speed.

"Crap!" I dodged to the left, but pain shot through the tip of my wing.

I plunged downward, a burning sensation ripping down my wing as my stomach lodged in my throat. The scent of singed feathers filled my nose as the pain increased.

"Shit! No!" The earth sped toward me. But just as quickly, my dark power rushed up, shooting through my body to my wings and halting the magical spell.

Gritting my teeth, I flapped my wings despite the searing pain flowing through the left one like molten lava.

My dark power coursed through my new appendage,

cooling the burning sensation even though the wing stayed charred. I flapped my wings more, catching a glimpse of the injured one.

Burned black feathers covered the top quarter of my wing, but my dark power had stopped the magic from destroying it further.

Flapping harder, I ascended slowly. My balance felt off, and I kept twisting. Gritting my teeth, I tried to adjust the strength of each flap to compensate for my damaged left wing.

Above me, Xanthia and Daniel fought valiantly, but like before, they couldn't beat Stephen, not while his protective barrier spell kept him safe.

Quaneely's belly shone cream-colored in the sun, the scales like a rough pearl. Fire continued to spew from her mouth.

Daniel dodged around each stream of fire as he tried unsuccessfully to get closer.

Since I was below them, Stephen couldn't see me.

A lightbulb turned on in my mind, and harsh determination followed. I flew faster, ascending in a vertical spiral. A moment of guilt about what I had to do flashed through me.

"I'm sorry," I whispered.

Even though Quaneely was one of hell's creatures, what she was doing wasn't of her own decision, and Xanthia loved her.

I only hoped my friend would forgive me.

I shot my hands up, my powers rushing to my palms as I climbed higher and higher in the sky. Quaneely's immense body loomed, her shorts legs folded against her belly.

Stephen didn't see me coming.

When I barreled into the dragon, my power was ready. Red light burst from my hands the second I made contact with the dragon's rough skin. I poured everything I had into it, not relenting when pain and heat made my palms glow crimson.

Quaneely screamed as my power tore through her, but I didn't let up, pushing and willing my angel powers to destroy the evil that dared ravage earth.

Stephen's shout of fear came right before the dragon exploded in the sky.

Chapter 26

Stephen plunged toward the ground, but the sorcerer somehow managed to use his magic to keep himself from dying when he landed, like a giant trampoline cushioned his fall. But he was no match for the twenty SF members who pounced on him—including Logan.

When Daniel, Xanthia, and I landed back on the ground, I breathed heavily, adrenaline making my heart pound.

I winced when the pain hit me. My charred left wing sagged at the tip, the beautiful white feathers wilted and black.

"Holy shit. Quaneely," Xanthia said, breathing heavily as she fell to her knees. "Quaneely . . ."

Guilt burned through me, doubling the pain from my

scorched wing.

"Use your powers to heal yourself." Daniel's wings receded back into his body, as if his shoulders had sucked them back inside, the skin healing over, and smooth muscle was once again all I could see.

I stared at Xanthia, wishing I hadn't had to kill Quaneely but not knowing what else I could have done to stop Stephen's destruction.

"Daria," Daniel said softly. He placed his palm between my shoulder blades, nestling it between my wings. Soothing power from him flowed into me, quenching some of the anxiety and guilt that threatened to fold me over. "Heal yourself, young angel."

Xanthia continued to face away from me, the dragon she'd been riding waiting in the nearby field.

I did as Daniel instructed, closing my eyes and working my powers together, the process similar to how I'd healed my ravaged body following Rigarion's assault.

When my wing tip sported healthy white feathers once again, Daniel taught me how to pull them back inside.

To say the process felt strange would be an understatement. In a way, my wings felt like life forces, just waiting to be called forth, but when I looked over my shoulder, nothing showed but my smooth skin and human-looking back.

"There. Well done," Daniel said quietly as I straightened my ripped shirt around me, thankful that my wings had sprouted through it, not shredding it from my body like Daniel's had done. For the most part, I was still covered.

I took a deep breath and coughed as ashy air filled my lungs.

Ahead of us, SF buildings continued to burn. The destruction spread far and wide.

I stepped toward Xanthia, pain again filling my insides. She stayed turned away, but I crouched at her side. "I'm sorry about Quaneely."

She didn't respond, and she didn't look at me.

"I didn't know how else to stop him," I added, my voice taking on a desperate tone.

"I know," she finally replied. "I understand why you did it, but . . ." She shrugged. "My dragons are like my babies, and Quaneely was a good dragon. She was only doing as I'd taught her, following the commands of her rider." Tears slipped from her eyes.

"I'm sorry," I whispered again. "I'm so sorry."

She just turned away more, still refusing to look me in the eye, and for the first time since meeting her, the cocky jut of her chin had disappeared.

Daniel stayed quiet, a step behind us.

"But the other two are safe, right?" I asked.

"Yeah." Her jaw locked as she wiped a tear from her cheek. "Roofessee and Drakon will be fine."

Rumblings and shouts came from the distance. Everyone was mobilizing since the battle was over.

"We'd better head back." I stood and offered Xanthia my hand.

She stood, not taking it. "Yeah. Let's go." She walked ahead of me, refusing to walk at my side.

My gut twisted, my chest tightening, but I didn't try to force anything.

When we arrived back at the base, Xanthia mumbled something about consulting with the sorcerers and witches about how to transport her dragons back to hell. She left before I could offer to help.

Daniel, however, turned toward me, his turquoise eyes filled with pride. "You've done well, young angel, better than I could have hoped for."

Heaviness about how Xanthia and I had parted still filled my chest, but I managed a small smile. "I have you to thank for that. Without your help, I don't think I ever would have learned how to live with my angel powers."

"But now you have. Your training isn't complete. You still have much to learn, but you're on your way, which is why I must leave you."

It felt as if the earth moved beneath me. "*What? Leave me? What are you talking about?*"

"Our maker has commanded I return home."

"He did? And you have to go *now?*"

"Yes, now."

"And you're going home to . . . heaven?"

Daniel smiled, that beautiful, more-dazzling-than-anything-on-earth smile. "Perhaps heaven or perhaps Emunda. I shall find out when I arrive."

I gripped his hand, my palms shaking. *First Xanthia, and now him? No! No! This isn't fair!*

It seemed too much to bear. I couldn't lose them both so quickly. Swallowing my sorrow, I asked him a question I'd always wondered. Anything to keep him talking. Anything to keep him staying on earth a little bit longer.

"What happened in the first place that got you kicked out of heaven?"

He smiled sadly. "I failed our maker. I was sent to retrieve a fallen angel, and I failed." The regret in his eyes hinted at how important his mission had been.

"I'm sure you tried as hard as you could."

Daniel dipped his head. "I did."

I stood rigidly, still grasping his hands. The scent of smoke filled my nose as squads and vehicles mobilized around us.

"Will I see you again?" Tears pricked my eyes.

"Fear not, young angel." He squeezed my hands. "Our kind never truly parts from one another." He leaned down and kissed me on the cheek, his lips as soft as velvet. "Now, I must go."

When he straightened, I pulled him into a fierce hug before he could disappear into thin air. "Please come back if you can. Please come to see me again if you're able."

His strong arms held me tight until I managed to swallow the tears that threatened to choke me. "Stay strong, young angel. Something tells me that we shall meet again. Until then, you must continue to do our maker's work while on earth."

I gave a small nod, my throat too constricted to speak further. I knew what he meant—I needed to return to my life as a supernatural healer and resume my purpose.

But where does that leave Logan and me?

"Goodbye, young angel."

I swallowed thickly. "Bye, Daniel."

Then he was gone.

∞ ∞ ∞

Over the next week, the SF pieced together how Stephen had created a portal between earth and hell. They wrangled that information from the remaining surviving demon-possessed supernaturals.

After constructing the portal, Stephen had recruited supernaturals who'd also wanted the SF gone. Each possessed supe had been a willing participant. They'd coexisted with their demons. Sometimes the demons were in charge, other times the supes were.

That fully explained Jayden's two sides and why he'd seemed normal when we met in the supermarket. At that time, Jayden—a rogue werewolf—had been in charge, not the demon.

And according to the demon-possessed, Stephen had indeed teamed up with a high-ranking demon in the underworld, one who had wanted to ultimately join him on earth. But Stephen hadn't been able to construct a portal to admit high-ranking demons, only low-ranking, yet the demon had been hoping with time that Stephen would be able to.

And once he did, the demon wanted to rule earth with Stephen at his side.

Their ultimate motive had been to destroy the SF. The Supernatural Forces was the only thing that could have thwarted the demon and Stephen's grand plan, and initially, Stephen had planned to kill as many SF members as possible—weakening the SF—before attacking the SF headquarters directly.

But when he learned of me and my growing abilities, he knew he needed to act fast. Angels were the only creatures who could truly destroy his plan.

After Logan told me all of that, I sat in silence. I found that information neither interesting nor surprising. Stephen's motive had been as old as time itself.

He'd wanted power and to rise to the top, removing the SF in the process, so he could govern a land of supernaturals without the consequence of law—the perfect recipe for a dictator's rise to power.

"So many lives lost and for what?" I whispered.

Logan nodded, sadness in his gaze. "But it's over and done with, and now we rebuild."

I held Logan's hand as he pulled me up. We were outside, among the ruined buildings and craters in the decimated SF headquarters. Makeshift refugee-style tents dotted the landscape since every barrack had been destroyed. Over a week had passed since the SF had defeated Stephen, but nobody was rejoicing despite our win.

Many lives had been lost.

Families had been torn apart.

It would take months to rebuild, but years of grief to move on.

I sniffled as the cool October wind flew against my cheeks, the sorcerer's weather-controlling spells too damaged to work properly. I thought of the two SF members I'd met who'd been killed when we strolled past the main headquarter building, which lay in ruins.

Millie, the kind, warm-hearted fairy who'd always had a smile for me when I entered the SF processing room, had died in one of the explosions.

And Holly, the witch who'd specialized in cloaking spells and had always had her eye on Logan, had been killed by a red-eyed vamp.

While Holly had never been someone I liked, I still grieved her death.

And Millie . . .

I would truly miss Millie.

Both of them had fought to protect the innocent supernaturals who lived on earth outside of the SF. They had given their lives to keep that freedom safe.

We wouldn't forget them.

"Have you heard from Xanthia?" Logan asked as we stepped over the ashy bricks covering the path.

"No. Not yet. I tried to reach out to her again this morning, but so far, she's never called me back." I frowned, my mood sinking more.

Xanthia had returned to California after securing her dragons back in hell, and the sorcerers and the fairies worked together to seal the portal that Stephen had constructed to allow the demons and dragons to ravage earth.

Logan squeezed my hand. "She'll come around. Sooner or later, things will be better between you two."

"Do you really think so? I killed one of her dragons.

They were like her children. Can someone really be forgiven for that?"

Logan's mouth thinned, his brow furrowing. "She's hurting right now, but she knows you did the right thing. Just give her time."

"I hope you're right."

He squeezed my hand again.

My skin glowed slightly in the afternoon sun. I'd been practicing my tempering daily. Slowly, I was getting better at it. Some days I didn't glow at all, but I missed not having Daniel to coach me. I hadn't heard from him either, which only made my mood bottom out.

But since I was learning to live with my angel powers, I knew that sooner or later, I would be able to return to my job. Nothing stopped me from returning to the life I'd once led, other than Logan, who'd ensnared my heart and completely rocked everything I knew about our world.

"So what happens now?" I asked when my bus came into sight.

Logan shrugged as his sandalwood scent floated around us. "Now, we rebuild and continue on. The Supernatural Forces has been in existence for hundreds of years. One battle isn't enough to ruin it, even though that was ultimately what Stephen had hoped for."

"No, I mean, what happens with *us?*"

That haunted look entered his eyes again. Over the past few days, when Logan and I weren't helping with cleanup, a tightened jaw and ragged expression had filled his face. Those moments were usually preceded by calls or text messages from someone back home.

He stopped to face me. "I won't give you up, Dar. I won't, but I can't hide in the SF anymore. I have to return home."

My throat constricted, tears filling my eyes. Pain filled me so deeply, I was drowning. Xanthia had shunned me. Daniel had left me. And now Logan was returning to his betrothed?

I couldn't bear it. I just couldn't.

I swallowed my tears. "To Crystal?"

"To everything. My scheduled wedding to her is coming up. Every day it grows closer."

"When is it?"

"The wedding's scheduled for three weeks. She's insisted the date be moved up. I thought I still had a few more months, but..."

I gasped. I'd known things were going on with Logan's pack and that he'd grown more agitated over the past few days, but I hadn't known *that* was why he'd become so irritable.

"Are you going to marry her?"

"No."

"But what about the Idaho pack? Won't that start a werewolf war?"

His only response was a tightening of his jaw, as his rich-brown eyes stared off in the distance.

Tears fell onto my cheeks. I could only hope it never came to that.

Chapter 27

One day later

The SF car's headlights cut through the night as Logan drove us deep into the mountains.

It was the first time either of us had left the SF following the destruction.

Cecile and Mike had both hugged me tightly before we left, not truly understanding all that I had gone through but trying to be there for me nonetheless.

"Where are we going?" I asked from the front passenger seat. Out my window, emerald trees and plants flashed by in a blur, growing darker in color as the sun dipped below the horizon.

Logan glanced over at me. "To a place I want to show

you."

I nibbled my fingernail as anxiety swirled in my belly. In the chaos that had ruled our lives since Stephen's attack, we hadn't been alone together—and tonight was the last night we had before Logan returned to his pack.

Fifteen minutes later, Logan pulled off the side of the narrow blacktop highway. Thick trees and dense brush filled the forest around us.

After he parked, we both stepped out of the car. The scent of pine hung in the air.

Since October had arrived, the temperature grew progressively cooler each night. I shivered and wrapped my arms around myself before grabbing my jacket.

Logan retrieved a backpack from the trunk. He slammed the trunk closed, the sound echoing up the empty road, before he swung the bag onto his back.

"What's in there?"

He just threaded his fingers through mine and pulled me toward the forest. "Come on."

I expected a trail, or something to follow, but all that waited before us was thick vegetation. I paused at the forest's edge. "Which way?"

He stepped closer before pulling me to him. The feel of his rock-hard chest pressing against mine had my nipples hardening before he swung me up in his arms. "I'll carry you."

He took off at a run, his breathing deep and even. The nighttime air caressed my cheeks. I closed my eyes, soaking up the feel of him and never wanting to let him go.

I knew Logan's upcoming responsibilities weighed heavily on his mind. All week he'd been cagey and tense, the call of his pack breathing up his neck like a raging fire even though he was intent on thwarting his responsibilities.

We climbed progressively higher and higher up the mountain, the air growing colder with each step.

A short while later, he stopped and set me down.

The moon shone down on us. Chilly air flowed over my skin as I took in our remote location. It was truly only him and me on the lone mountaintop.

A break in the forest opened directly in front of me, a steep cliff plunging down the mountainside. The break allowed a perfect view of the dark emerald forest and the starry sky.

"It's beautiful," I said.

He leaned down and gently kissed me on the neck. "I think so too." He trailed his lips lower, pressing soft kisses to my collarbone.

His warm breath made shivers wrack my body. I leaned to the side, giving him better access to my neck. Goose bumps erupted across my flesh.

Logan's hands gripped my hips, pulling my ass closer to him. I sucked in a breath when I felt his erection.

He pulled back and slipped off his backpack. "Are you hungry?" His voice caught at the end, hinting at his deep emotions that he was trying valiantly to hide.

I shook my head, that anxious feeling swirling in my stomach again.

He unzipped the bag and withdrew two large, thick

blankets. He spread one of the blankets out on the ground.

"Come here." He trailed his hands up my sides. I shivered when his palms grazed over my breasts before settling on the buttons in the middle of my shirt. My nipples hardened, standing to attention for him like proud soldiers.

He dipped his head again and kissed the side of my neck as he slowly undid each button.

One by one, my shirt opened before him, my breasts straining to be free.

When he spread my shirt, cool air washed over my abdomen before he pulled me closer to him, my shirt slipping off behind me.

My near-naked chest pressed against his clothed one as he leaned down. His lips parted mine, his tongue dancing into my mouth. I moaned against him. He tasted delicious, like honey and spice, and I clung to him like it was the last night we had on earth.

He pulled back, only enough to pull his shirt over his head, before his arms were around me again, his hot fingers trailing up and down my spine.

I shivered, the urge to squirm and grind against him growing stronger by the second. He was leaving in the morning, yet he didn't want to leave me, and I didn't want to leave him, but neither of us knew what the future truly held.

His fingers danced higher as we continued to kiss and taste. Light feathery touches from his hands moved around my bra's clasp, then it was free and falling from my shoulders.

My breasts spilled out of the flimsy material, full and heavy, as my nipples ached and grew taut, begging for his touch.

"Touch me," I whispered. "I want to feel you. I *need* to feel you."

Whatever loomed in the future for Logan and I had grown more imminent each day.

Duty called to us both.

A duty that could pull us apart.

He wrenched me to him, and our mouths met again as we fell onto the blanket. Logan cushioned the blow, catching me just before he lowered me down and then pressed himself on top of me. Somehow, we both rid ourselves of our jeans. I gasped when his cock sprang free, instinctively reaching for it while I parted my thighs.

He settled between me, and I raised my legs while encircling his hard length with my hand. I rubbed my palm up and down his shaft, marveling at his velvety steel.

He hissed and shut his eyes. "It's been too long. I've wanted you all week." Sweat beaded on his forehead as he pushed against my entrance. "I've longed to feel you again, to hear you moan, hear you cum, to make you *mine*."

"Yes." I arched against him, urging him to penetrate my sex.

He moved into me inch by inch until he filled my core and stretched me in mind-blowing bliss.

When his hard length was fully settled within me, he began to thrust with deep, aching movements.

"You're mine, Dar. I won't let you go."

I clung to him tightly. With each thrust, my muscles quivered and tensed. His cock slid deep inside me, rubbing my core and demanding that I respond. I moaned again, my heels digging into his ass as the waves began to build.

"So sweet," he murmured and thrust again. "So beautiful."

He picked up the pace, moving faster and faster, an intense glow brightening his eyes as I arched more, my movements growing frantic as I clung to him and raked my fingernails up and down his back.

He groaned, his biceps straining as his cock grew even thicker inside me. His nostrils flared as an orgasm threatened to shatter me.

"That's it, babe. Cum for me. I want to hear you scream."

I gripped his shoulders tightly and lost all sense of time as my singular thought became the feel of Logan's length and the building pressure that wouldn't cease.

He gripped my waist, and the veins in his neck bulged as I matched his movements, my hips rising to meet his thrusts as the wave built higher inside me.

"Now, Dar," he groaned. "Cum now!"

He slammed into me, and an earth-shattering orgasm rocked through my core. I screamed and bucked as a fierce growl tore from Logan's throat. He pumped into me with one final blow before his hips seized and he shouted his release.

His hot seed spilled inside my sex, and I relished the

feel as my body shuddered in his arms. He held me to him, cherishing me, protecting me. I kept my arms wrapped tightly around him, never wanting to let him go.

Minutes ticked by, and our breathing slowed. A chill ran over me as a starry night stretched across the sky above us. Logan's cock softened inside me before he pulled out and gathered me in his arms. He hauled me against him, offering me his warmth, before pulling the second blanket up.

I settled in the crook of his arm, pressing soft kisses to his chest. "It's a good thing I'm on birth control now," I whispered. I'd consulted the SF witches, and they'd given me a potion. One potion drink per month, and conception wasn't possible.

Logan smiled sadly as he gazed at me with his dark eyes.

It was a bittersweet moment since in a month I may no longer need that potion.

I closed my eyes and threaded my fingers through his. I didn't want the moment to end as the cool nighttime wind swirled around us, and sweat from our lovemaking dried on our skin. But I also knew that we couldn't hide from our responsibilities forever. I still had sick clients to heal, he was still the future alpha of his pack, and Crystal waited.

No mountaintop could hide us from those facts.

"What time do you go back?" I whispered.

The strong *lub-dub* of his heart filled his chest as a ragged breath sucked into his lungs. "First thing in the morning."

My throat tightened, and I forced a swallow as tears threatened to fill my eyes. "So is this it then? Was this your way of saying goodbye?"

His grip tightened. "Hell no. I'm not going without you." His tone turned low and harsh. "I want you to come with me. I want you to stay at my side."

I closed my eyes, remembering what my mother and my nan had taught me—what Daniel had taught me.

I was a Gresham.

My purpose was to heal, not to chase a life of self-gratification, and I still had questions that needed answering, ones that had nothing to do with Logan.

Where had my family's ring gone, and what did it do? What else did the psychic know? Where had that voice come from in my mind while I'd been in Rigarion? How had my distant witch grandmother met an archangel if angels weren't allowed on earth?

But those answers would have to wait for another day.

I swallowed back my tears. "I can't run from my calling either, Logan. Eventually, I'll need to leave you, even if I join you at your home tomorrow."

His jaw locked, his grip around me growing harder. "I know, but I can't let you go, Dar. I just can't."

I squeezed him back, but even I knew that sometimes wishes didn't come true, and although we'd defeated Stephen and the SF was safe once again, the upcoming battle that Logan and I faced had only just begun.

Continue the Story

Angel in Embers, the final book in the Supernatural Community series.

www.kristastreet.com

Thank you for reading *Dragons in Fire,* book three in the Supernatural Community series!

If you enjoy Krista Street's writing, make sure you join her newsletter at **www.kristastreet.com** to stay up-to-date on new releases, book deals, and all of the writing stuff she's up to.

And if you enjoyed *Dragons in Fire,* please consider logging onto Amazon to post a review. Authors rely heavily on readers reviewing their work. Even one sentence helps a lot. Thank you so much if you do!

♥

To learn more about Krista's other books and series, visit her website. Links to all of her books, along with links to her social media platforms, are available on every page.

About the Author

Krista Street is a Minnesota native but has lived throughout the U.S. and in another country or two. She loves to travel, read, and spend time in the great outdoors. When not writing, Krista is either spending time with her family, sipping a cup of tea, or enjoying the hidden gems of beauty that Minnesota has to offer.

Printed in Great Britain
by Amazon